LOVING CHARLEY
(FULL CIRCLE #3)

by Casey Peeler

D1563786

DISCARD

Acknowledgements:

Special thanks to:

My husband, Billy, and daughter, Carlee, thank you for being there on this adventure. I love you both with my whole heart!

My sister, Pam Baldwin, at Paperclutch for the cover design. You have always been there at any given moment. Cover one was an adventure for both of us, cover two was a breeze, and three full of choices! It is as fabulous as you! Love you!

My parents, Mike and Cindy, thanks for believing in me like you always do! Parental support is important no matter your age!

Jeannette & Mike thank you for your judicial expertise!

Chelly Peeler, you've had my back from day one. You have helped keep up with reviews at Hardcover Therapy while I finished writing, read *NTB, FC, & LC*, read it again, edited, and given advice. We aren't just family; you truly are one of my best friends, and I couldn't have done this without you.

My Boondock Betas, thank you so much for your thoughts and feelings that have brought this book to life. I owe y'all!

Paige, you have read, edited, read, edited, read,

and edited! I couldn't have done this without you! Round three has been amazing! I can't wait to continue our editing journey!

Southern Charms, my street team, y'all are sweet as sugar! I honestly wouldn't be where I am today without you! With each like, share, comment, and review, you've gone above and beyond each and every day! I <3 y'all!

Cortlan Allen, my cover model, thank you for taking part in this journey from start to finish.

Brian Harris at Firelight Photography for the cover photos.

My family, friends, authors, and bloggers, thanks for your thoughts, posts, shares, tweets, and likes!

*For Chelly, who's been with me on this journey
since it was a thought, and now it's come full circle!*

Table of Contents

Previously in *Finding Charley*

"Somebody help me! PLEEEAASSSSSEEEE!" I expel from my lungs. No one. Not a soul sees us. My adrenaline kicks into high gear. I put the Ariats in the wind and haul ass to the fire.

As the roar of the fire comes into view, so do all the people. They are oblivious to what has just occurred. They continue to sing, drink, and party as I run as fast as I can. The more people I'm around, the safer I am. I see Piper and Joe sitting on a log. A look of horror flashes when she sees me, and her eyes speak volumes. I know that he is coming…that he is coming for me… it's time to face the devil with everyone watching. Knowing that I don't want to turn around and face him, I center my feelings to my core, and I do it anyway.

Dylan is within a few feet of me. He has a mix of emotions on his face that include shock, pain, and confidence, but the obvious one is rage.

"Stay away from me," I growl through my teeth.

He laughs wickedly as he inches closer. "I'll never stay away. Don't you get it? You're mine." Grabbing my waist, he pulls me close to him. I try to escape his clutch, but it's impossible. "You were mine from the first time I saw you at GPAC."

For the first time, all eyes fall on us. Dylan is about to be famous, but not in a good way.

"Like hell I was!" I say as a lean back from him.

"You are so full of shit, Charley! You know you wanted me, everyone does, but I made sure of it! That state championship made you fall hard. You were different, like a new event at a meet that I was going to win, and then I sealed the deal at Trent's. You fell for it so easily. I slipped that "Z" in your beer without you knowing. You were so naïve and stupid! Going to the bathroom was just classic!"

People begin to whisper and point, as we are on full display now. Something inside me snaps. I push him back, but he comes at me again. This time I can't push him off me, and I struggle to stand my ground. I use every ounce of force, but as soon as I'm ready to push away again, a fist comes in contact with his jaw. Cash.

Punch after punch, blow after blow, Cash continues to take out the past eighteen months of bottled-up emotions on him. Cash continues to hit him over and over. The sounds coming from Dylan's body are like none I have ever heard. There are cracks, crunches, whimpers, and howls. By the time Cash is finished, Dylan is lying in a fetal position in the dirt, not moving.

"You listen to me, motherfucker. Char-coal's not yours. She's mine."

Chapter 1

Dylan doesn't move. He just lies there... motionless. *Oh God, is he dead?* Dustin leaves Tessa and rushes to his side like the brother he should be. My heart begins to race, and I'm terrified of what just happened. As I glance around, I notice everyone's eyes are focused on us. For a while, Cash stands there like he is glued in one spot and then slowly begins to walk backward from Dylan and toward me. I want to speak, shout from the rooftops to tell everyone to quit staring at me, but nothing... not a damn word escapes my lips.

"Char-coal, let's get the hell outta here," Cash says firmly while looking over to Dustin. Dustin looks up at Cash and nods with assurance that he will try to keep the repercussions to a bare minimum. "Char, did you hear me?" I'm still frozen.

Before I have time to think, Cash engulfs my body, picking me up in one swift move. As I semi begin to snap out of shock, I see Tessa and the Kluft girls gathering their things and following behind us.

Once we reach the truck, Cash boosts me into the passenger side before hustling around to the driver's side. After he closes the door and cranks the truck, I slide as close as possible to him. I look up into his eyes and say the only words that I can mutter, "Thank you, Cash Money."

"There's no need to thank me, Char-coal. He's had that comin' for a long time now, but I'm pretty sure this isn't the end of it."

Removing myself from his right side, I glance at him with a questioning look. "What do you mean?" He uses his right hand to put the truck in reverse, but pauses as pain flashes across his face. I see that his right hand is beginning to swell and has a knot the size of a golf ball on it. "Ohmygosh! We've got to take you to the hospital." He laughs as he uses his left hand to put the truck in gear. "What's so funny?" I ask.

"Do you know what will happen if I go to the hospital? I'm pretty sure that Dylan's gonna end up there, and it's not gonna take a genius to put the puzzle pieces together."

At that moment, the impact of this entire situation has come to the forefront. I now know that this plan was a mistake, not only for me, but also for everyone I love. There is no way that I am going to be able to fix this, but I'm going to try my best, even if it kills me.

Chapter 2

Once we enter town, my phone starts blowing up. The Kluft girls need to know what to do and where to go, Tessa's an absolute wreck, and Piper and Joe are on our heels. Without thinking, I do the one thing that I should have done a long time ago. "Cash, it's time."

"Time for what?"

"It's time to go downtown. I need to talk to the police before they come after you. I can't let you go down for my mess."

"Char-coal, no! Regardless, I'm gonna get in trouble, but you are not putting yourself through this. I don't want you to have to keep reliving this."

"Don't you get it? I'm always gonna relive this! Until I tell the truth, it's not going to end. Please, I'm begging you! You've protected me for so long; it's my turn now. Let me be the one to rescue you like you have done for me as long as I can remember."

As we get closer to the center of town, I'm positive that Cash is going to keep driving and not stop. "Cash, if you don't stop now, I'm coming back as soon as you drop me off. It's better off if we do this together. Remember, Char-coal plus Cash Money equals forever." I take his swollen hand in mine.

"Are you sure? Once we do this, there is no turning back, ya know?"

"I know."

"Things will be different, people are going to talk, and your parents will know it all."

"It's time." With those two words, Cash makes a left-hand turn for the police station. I send Piper, Tessa, and Georgia a brief text. I'm a mess of emotions. *Can I really do this? Is this what I want? What will happen to Cash? What are my parents going to think?* But as we pull into the station, I'm only one emotion—calm. Just like the eye of a hurricane or the calm before the storm. I know that things are going to be a battle from this moment forward, but it's one I'm ready to fight until the end.

He puts the truck in park with his left hand and turns off the ignition. I see Piper and Joe pull into the space beside us. Cash looks at me, and I fall into those eyes of his. No words are spoken at first because I can read his thoughts. We are walking in together, but I doubt we will be walking out the same. Placing my hands on his scruffy cheek, I place my lips slowly on his as the tears stream down my face.

Knowing time isn't on our side, we pull ourselves apart. "I love you, Cash Money, and no matter what happens, I'm here. We will come out on top. Now, let's get this over with."

He opens his door and slides out, and I follow right behind him. Piper and Joe are getting out of the car as well. "I think y'all might need to go on to the farm. This is about to be a mess, and I need someone there with Tessa."

I hear a strong, yet sweet, voice behind me. "No one needs to check on Tessa because I'm not going home." I turn around, and we meet each other in the middle. "Char, I wasn't there when it happened, but I'm sure as hell not gonna let you do this without me."

"What about the Kluft girls? Did they just drop you off?" Then, I see them, sitting in the distance near Tori's Explorer. "Any word from Dustin?"

"I know they are on their way to Trent's. I'm pretty sure Dylan doesn't want to go to the hospital, but I bet he's gonna have to. Cash whooped his ass, and it's about damn time!"

"Yeah, he did, but I gotta take care of this before Dylan gets admitted or Cash could get in big trouble."

I turn from Tessa, but do a one-eighty. I pull her in for a hug and tell her thank you before grabbing the hand of the man I love and walking into the police station.

Chapter 3

Opening the glass doors to the Grassy Pond police station is kind of surreal. As I walk inside these doors, it feels as if it is a dream. I'm going to wake up from this nightmare, and everything will be how it should have been before Dylan. Once the glass closes behind us and a middle-aged woman with glasses asks how she can help us, I'm brought back to reality. No, this isn't a dream. I'm awake and in the moment.

"I need to file a report."

Adjusting her glasses, she punches a few keys on the computer. "Name?"

"Charley Anne Rice." She pauses and looks at me.

"As in the Rice farm?"

"Yes, ma'am." Cash places his hand on my lower back. I glance and smile at him.

"I went to school with your daddy. What type of report are we looking into filing?"

"Rape." She stops mid-type and gives a *deer in the headlights* look. Undoubtedly, this isn't something they hear a lot of in Grassy Pond.

"Miss Rice, are you sure?"

"Yes, ma'am." She asks me basic information, and then we sit and wait. The lobby area is cold and musty smelling. After what feels like an eternity, an officer appears from behind a wooden door.

"Miss Rice, this way, please."

Cash and I stand. Hand in hand, we make our way to the officer. He takes us back to his office and offers me a seat. Taking a deep breath, I explain everything that occurred eighteen months ago. Cash's hand never leaves mine, and the officer listens while taking notes.

Once I finish reliving my real life nightmare, the officer folds his hands and places them on his desk.

"Miss Rice, you understand that once this charge is filed, there is no going back. I'm not sure exactly what will come of this, due to the time frame and his word against yours, but you need to be prepared. This town isn't going to take lightly to these types of accusations, especially against Dylan Sloan. I've seen him swim, and he's got a fan club in this town.

"Yes, sir. I know I should have come forward a long time ago, but who's gonna believe 'Mr. Can't-Do-Anything-Wrong' raped me? Cash tried to get me to, but I wouldn't. The rape was awful, but his control and presence is the real problem. I just want him to leave me and everyone else alone."

"I understand. I haven't been in your situation, but the allegations are serious. Once I submit this report, things might get ugly. I'm not sayin' you shouldn't; just be prepared." Turning, he looks at Cash. "Mr. Montgomery, do you understand that if Dylan Sloan comes to press charges against you, you will have consequences to face?"

"Yes, sir."

"Officer, I have a question? What if I file my report based off the stalker like conduct? I have evidence."

"As in what type of evidence?"

"Sir, I have a box with photos that he had taken of me, phone records, and Facebook messages. The list is a mile long."

"Miss Rice, it is totally up to you, but if you want him to stay away, you need to file a restraining order. We will need the evidence, but I wouldn't let the other charge go. You never know what the court will decide, and you just might save another girl's life. As for you, Mr. Montgomery, I need a statement from you about tonight's events."

Cash gives his statement to the officer, and once he is finished, we are dismissed except for bringing the evidence back to the station as soon as possible.

As we walk out into the lobby, Piper, Tessa, and Joe stand. About that time, the receptionist informs the officer that charges are planning to be filed from the Grassy Pond Medical Center. We all look at each other and realize this is about to get dirty.

"Cash, let's get that box now."

"You got it."

As we walk back to the truck, the Kluft girls are waiting. I tell them to follow us to the farm, but we have a lot to do in a short amount of time. I snuggle up to Cash as close as possible. I have no idea what is about to happen, but I know that it is going to involve the devil in human form, my knight in an F250, my parents, my friends, and half of this town if I'm not careful.

As if Cash is reading my mind, he kisses the top of my head. "It's gonna be fine, Char-coal. I promise."

"I know, but it's what we have to get through until the 'fine' part that I'm worried about."

We remain quiet for the remainder of the ride to the farm. Once we turn onto the gravel road, I know I have to make a decision—talk to my parents, get the box of evidence, or act like this didn't happen.

Cash puts the truck in park. "You ready?" I nod.

"Cash Money, I love you more than life itself." I crash my lips into his because it could be our last kiss for an extremely long time.

Cash pulls away from me. "Don't do this, Char-coal. This isn't the end; it's the beginning.

Remember, we're in this forever. Now, let's go get that box!"

As I open the door, I'm greeted by the Kluft girls, Joe, Piper, and Tessa.

"Hey, y'all. We've gotta get something from the club. I need y'all to keep my parents occupied until we get back. Then, I got some explainin' to do."

"I've got ya covered, Sis," Tessa says, but not before Hayden puts in her two cents.

"Tessa, we've got this! We've got Mama and Papa Rice under control. Let's just say we can get her talking, and she's not gonna stop. Your dad will be stuck listening."

We have a quick group hug; the girls walk toward the house while Tessa, Piper, and Joe follow us to the club. We make our way to the barn before grabbing a shovel and getting on the Gator, and then we put the pedal to the metal.

Once we get to the club, Cash turns off the Gator, but leaves on the lights. He takes my hand in his while I grab the shovel.

"Um, we'll just wait here," Tessa informs us.

"It's okay if y'all wanna get a little dirty."

"Char, this isn't a time to be funny!" Piper says smartly.

Ignoring Piper, I turn to Cash. "We've gotta get something on that hand when we get back."

"I know," he says, looking at his swollen hand.

They stay at the Gator, and we walk to the club. There is no need for a flashlight because the headlights shine directly onto the spot below the club. Cash tries to take the shovel from me, but I shake him off. He knows this is about me. Yes, his hand is near broken, but this is what I have to do.

Within four digs, I strike gold... I'd guess you'd say. Bending down to my knees, I scrape the excess dirt from the top of the box and remove it from the earth. The fact that it hasn't been buried too long has helped from ruining the evidence. I stand and begin to walk toward the Gator.

"Char-coal, aren't you going to open it?"

"Hell no. I know what's in there."

Cash has a pleading stare in his eyes.

"Please look, Char-coal. Who knows, he could have been damn Houdini and made it vanish."

"Seriously?" I ask Cash as he nods. "Fine."

Once we get to the Gator and are seated, I open the box.

"See... it's all here." Everything is within the box, but as Joe looks at the contents, his face loses color.

"Hey Joe, you aight?" I ask.

"Um, yeah. I'm just kinda worried. I mean, what do you think will happen to me since I knew about it all? Dammit! I can't get arrested. I'll lose everything Gran and I worked for."

"Look, I'll do my best to make sure nothing happens to you, Joe. Just like Cash, I'm not letting you take the blame for what that asshole did. Damn, I wish someone had gotten that shit on video. You'd think that with technology these days somebody would have gotten it, but noooo, they were too busy staring."

"Thank you, Squirrel. Gran is gonna kill me no matter what."

"Can we get going? Just lookin' at that box is freakin' me out," Piper says.

In unison we agree and make our way back to the house. As we approach, I'm unsure if I can do this. Walking into that station was one thing, but delivering this box to them will start a ball rolling that can create an avalanche.

As if being mind readers, Cash puts his hand on my knee while Tessa places her hand on my shoulder. Their love and support are amazing.

"Tess, have you heard from Dustin? Is Dylan going to survive?"

"Yeah, he said that he had a few broken ribs, but was going to make it. He might have to stay a few days, though. Cash fucked him up, and he's a damn puss. Mr. Big-and-Bad, but whimpers like a damn baby. Cash, I'm glad you beat the shit outta him because if I had to go along with this plan much longer, it might have been me." I roll my eyes as she continues. "I see that, Char! Dustin's okay, too, but he said his parents were pissed. I don't know what all this will do to us," Tessa says.

I whip my head around. "What do you mean? I mean, I know things will be weird, but you and Dustin are perfect for each other."

"I agree, but it's going to be hard. I just don't know if we will survive. We're not as strong as Cash and you."

I don't know what to say, so I say nothing. Once we are at the front porch, I start to fidget with the top of the box. Cash stops me as the others go inside. He takes my arm and turns me around while trying to move my hair from my face with his swollen hand.

"Hey, are you okay? I mean… really okay?" I bite my lip and shake my head yes. "You know that I'm not leaving. I'll tell as much as you want me to or keep it quiet if you want." Leaning in, he kisses my forehead and lets his lips linger for a few extra seconds.

We don't separate each other's hands as we walk to the house. Feeling like I'm in slow motion, I count the steps going up the porch, one…two… three…four. Cash pulls on the screen door, and it squeaks as he opens it. It's time to tell everything.

Chapter 4

Walking into my house has a different feeling at this point. I can hear Hayden talking above the others, and I think they might be playing cards. There is absolutely no telling.

Cash glances in my direction. "I love you, Char-coal."

"I love you more, Cash Money," I say as he wraps his arm around my waist.

We head into the kitchen where everyone is sitting with a few cards, but Dad is stuck with about one hundred. Bless him. They aren't going to let him win.

"Charley, glad y'all made it in. Whatcha got there?" Mama asks while peering at the box.

"Um… well… I think we need to talk, but first I need to get Cash some ice."

Everyone's eyes fall on Cash's hand as he removes it from behind me.

"Boy, what the hell happened? Hope whoever you got in a fight with looks worse than you do," Dad states.

Setting the box onto the counter, I go to the freezer, and grab an icepack for Cash. Once I've placed the icepack on his hand, I pick the box back up, and we make our way to the table.

Mama looks at Dad, and the Kluft girls look around, unsure if they should stay or go. Tori begins to stand, but I shake my head no. I want them here. Everyone needs to know the entire truth.

"Char, I think it would be better if you talked to your parents alone first," Tori says.

"I understand that, but I only want to tell this once."

"Well, if you want us to leave at any time, just say the word."

My mama's face is white as a ghost. She has known deep in her heart for a long time that something was going on, but I've never been brave enough to tell the details.

As we approach the table, everyone scoots in, and we take our seat with Cash by my side, as usual. Gradually, I move the box onto the table.

All eyes are on me, but before I open the box, I speak to my parents. "Mama and Dad, there are some things you don't know about me, Dylan, Cash, and pretty much everyone at this table. I've kept a secret, but it's time to tell. Please let me say everything I need to before you jump to conclusions, and once I say what I have to, things will change... but how I want them to. Okay?"

Dad doesn't say a word, but sits there with his arms crossed. Mama looks at me for direction.

"Remember when y'all had to go to that sale in Athens and left me at home?" They both nod. "Well, something bad happened that night. Dylan put something in my drink, and let's just say he took advantage of me." I can tell that my parents are putting the pieces together and are dying to speak. I lift my finger to tell them to just let me talk. Tears begin to roll down my mama's cheeks.

"Mama, don't cry. I'm all right. Cash saved me that night. Besides Dylan, he's the only one that knows the entire story. If it wasn't for him, I don't know what would have happened to me. I did the only thing I knew how to do; I pushed everyone away—the team, my friends, and y'all. I just survived. Yes, I'm different, but I'm okay." As I take a breath, it gives my mama a chance to speak.

Anger begins to rise in her eyes. "Charley, you mean to tell me that Dylan Sloan raped you, and you went out with him again? He was in this house this week. What the hell was that about?"

My mama never cusses.

"I'm telling you there is more to this story. I've dealt with what happened to me thanks to Tessa, Cash, and my friends. Going to Southern was the best choice I could have made. What I didn't know was how Dylan wasn't going to let me go. He's been keeping tabs on me since I went to school by taking pictures, sending messages to Joe, and even having Joe work for him." As soon as those words come out of my mouth, my dad is standing from his chair and holding Joe by his collar.

"Son, you better explain real quick, or I'll be serving your ass to the hogs!"

I jump up and make my way to Dad and Joe. "Dad! Put him down! He's not like Dylan. He just got caught up in trying to be his friend. I promise!"

"Charley, if I let go of him and he's done something to hurt my girl, he better run like hell."

"Dad, I promise. He's a good guy."

Dad lets Joe go. He walks cautiously to his side of the table again and sits, but never removes his eyes from Joe.

"Joe met Dylan during Senior Week at Myrtle Beach. They kept in contact, and when Dylan heard I was going to Southern, he asked Joe to keep an eye on me. Joe didn't realize that we were broken up. He just thought he was being a good friend to Dylan. Within twenty-four hours of meeting me, he knew that something was off, but continued to do what Dylan asked. He knew nothing about Dylan drugging me, and when I confessed everything to him, he was in complete shock. He was too deep in lies to tell the truth until Study Day. He told me that Dylan was the one behind it all, but that was really to protect me. Dylan had pictures taken of me at school. He even had pictures of Piper at school. I still can't put my finger on that, but I know that if Joe hadn't told me he was involved that night, I might not be alive today."

"What do you mean 'alive today'?" Mama questions.

"Dylan would have been at Whiskey River that night, the same place we were going. I don't know if he would have tried the same stunt again or something worse. The truth is, when Joe ripped my heart apart that night, I thought it was the end of the world. It wasn't until I was home for break that I found out the reason why."

"I have one question for you, Charley." Mama pauses. "Why did you fall all over Cash then push him away and go out with Dylan?" Nothing like Mama to just cut to the chase.

I look into Cash's eyes as he wraps his arm around my shoulder.

"This happened over a year ago. I didn't want the world to know, but I wanted it to stop. The only way for it to stop was for me to put the joke on him, which I did tonight, I might add, thanks to all of y'all. But I had to make you believe that Cash and I were through."

Dad grins, and I wonder what he is thinking, especially with what I just unloaded on him.

"Charley, it was a good stunt, but your mama and I knew that it wasn't over. Hell, it's just beginning between y'all two. We just thought you were being a reckless teenager."

Rolling my eyes, I focus back on the story. "I wanted to let everyone in Grassy Pond know what he did, make him fall for me, and make him famous in a small town… and not in a good way either. He fell for it hook, line, and sinker. There were a few glitches and surprises for both sides along the way, but we took him down tonight."

"So, that explains this," Mama says, pointing to Cash's hand.

"Yes, ma'am," he replies.

"Things didn't go quite like I planned tonight, and he is still the same asshole he has always been, but he told on himself in front of God and everybody. I just wish someone had gotten it on video. My only concern now is what is going to happen to Cash. You know Dylan's gonna file some assault charges or something."

"Char-coal, I told you not to worry about that. If I have to do time, it will be well worth it."

"Don't talk like that! You aren't going to jail. I won't let them. Not after what he did to me."

We sit in silence for a moment before I remove the lid from the box and pour the contents onto the table. Everyone's eyes are enormous, and Piper begins to cry.

"Ohmygosh, Char! How? How did he do this? No one is at my school with me? How?"

I start to speak, but Joe interrupts me. "Pipe, Dylan is a piece of work. He has little spies everywhere. For example, I had nothing to do with these pictures either. I knew something was going on, but this one of Charley and me, I didn't do it. I'm pretty sure who did, though. It's someone that I'm close to in living quarters, if you get my drift? Matt is always where we are, even if it's behind the scenes. I can't prove it, but I'll figure it out when I get back."

"What do we do now?" Mama asks.

"Well, tonight, after Cash beat Dylan to a pulp, we left the party and went to the police. I knew that if I didn't tell my side first, Cash wouldn't stand a chance. I'll be filing a restraining order for starters. That's why we came to get the evidence. I don't know if I want to file rape charges against him, though. It's been over a year, no evidence, and my word against his. Personally, I just want his name and swimming career ruined and to get my life back and move on. I love Grassy Pond, but I know I'll never be able to move back here with him haunting me."

"Charley, I think you should take that to the station now. Don't wait until the morning. I'll go with you," Dad says.

"Yes, sir, but what about Cash?"

29

We take a moment to let things soak in. This is it.

"Don't worry about me, but I do need to talk to my parents. I'll be glad to go back to the station with you."

Oh my gosh! What are his parents going to think? They are going to know that I'm tainted in the worst way possible and have been a complete bitch to Cash in front of everyone in town, but yet, I love him. I didn't think this plan through at all. The only thing I have going for me is that they know me.

"Cash, if you want to go, that is fine, but you need to call your mama before we leave. If the police come lookin' for ya, they need to hear it from you first."

"Yes, sir." With that, Cash pulls out his phone and calls home.

Chapter 5

Once Cash talks to his mama, who is livid about the situation because we can hear her through the phone, we make our way to my dad's truck. It's a quiet ride to the station.

As Dad goes to grab the door handle, he stops and looks at me.

"Charley, whatever happens in there, I want you to know that your mama and I support you. I really want to take the shotgun over to Dylan's and blow his head off, but I know that won't solve anything. You are makin' the right decision. I just wish you had told us. We would have been with you every step of the way."

"I know, but at the time I just didn't know what to do. I know they aren't going to be able to do anything about the rape, but I just want to be left alone."

"We will make sure that happens, sweet girl."

We exit the truck and walk toward the station. As we enter the glass doors, I hold the box tighter. The lady glances up from her desk to start the "Hey, I haven't seen you in years" speech with Dad. He cuts her off quickly, and we wait for the officer again.

The wooden door opens, and the officer appears.

"Miss Rice, glad to see you so soon. Right this way. I take it this is your dad, correct?"

"Yes, sir."

I feel like I'm on replay, just Dad is with me this time. He wants answers, what do we do next, and how are we going to get this situation under control. The officer takes a moment to think and then responds.

"Miss Rice, there are some things I need to make you aware of at this time. Have you heard of the statute of limitations?" I shake my head no. "Basically, that is the time frame for reporting a crime. Due to the nature of the crime you are reporting, we can't gather evidence. We have verbal witnesses, but that would not stand up in court. It would be very messy. Do you understand what I'm saying?"

I start to answer, but Dad interrupts. "So, you mean to tell me that since Charley didn't report this in a *timely manner* nothing can be done? What is this world comin' to?"

"Sir, I understand your concern, and I'm not going to say that I believe that it is right, but it's the law. Miss Rice does have one ball in her court. She can file charges against Dylan for stalking or threatening phone calls. Can I see what's in the box?"

"Yes, sir," I answer.

I take the box from my lap and pass it to the officer. He removes the pictures and looks through them one by one. Just looking at them wouldn't mean much to someone, but the fact that we didn't know about them and then mailing them to me was his mistake.

"You don't know who took these pictures?"

"No, sir, but they were mailed to me around my birthday. The card should say enough. It is in there."

The officer quickly reads the card and agrees.

"What else do you have?" he asks.

"We have Facebook messages and texts."

"Miss Rice, you have plenty of evidence, and I feel that your best action will be to complete a civil no-contact order often referred to as a 50C. Once it is filled out, Mr. Sloan will be notified and placed on a temporary 50C until the judge can decide. He won't be able to come near you."

"Okay, I guess that's what we should do." I answer all the officer's questions while filling out the 50C. The fact that as soon as I walk out of these doors my life will change is freeing. I do worry about Cash and what will happen with his situation, but I'm more worried about Tessa. She loves Dustin, and this is definitely going to complicate things.

While we are finishing the paperwork, I get a text. Uncertain if I should look, I glance at Cash who takes my phone and has a puzzled look on his face.

"Everything okay?"

"Um, you might want to take a look at this, Char-coal." I excuse myself from the officer and look. I can't believe my own eyes. Tessa has texted me with a link to the fight. This shit is all over the Internet. Relief washes over me, and I now know exactly what I have to do. Dylan is getting more than a damn restraining order, if I can help it.

"Officer, I have a question. If I have him admitting what he did to me, how would things change?"

He puts down his pencil, and I can see a little bit of irritation, but I can't blame him. I'd hate to have to fill out something else, too. He takes my phone and watches the video. Unable to read his reaction, I'm unsure of what he is going to say.

"Ma'am, I do believe the big man upstairs is on your side. This changes things entirely. No longer will you need a 50C. You now need a 50B, and we can file charges for second-degree rape. " He pauses before turning to Cash. "Mr. Montgomery, get ready because this is a double-edged sword for you. The Sloans can use this against you as well."

The inner happiness that I was beginning to feel soon deflates when he speaks his last words. I begin to shake my head no.

Dad looks at Cash, the officer, and me. "Excuse me, officer. I think we might need to give them a minute," Dad says, and they leave us alone for a moment.

Brushing my hair behind my ear, Cash tells me, "Char-coal, you have to. There's no other way. I'm prepared to pay the price. Every moment that I have to pay will be worth the day when I can walk out and hold you in my arms forever with no chance of Dylan Sloan ever hurting you or another girl again."

Cash's words, "another girl," ring in my ears. That's what this is really about—saving another girl from this asshole. Tears begin to stream down my face, and as much as I just want to take the easy way out, I can't.

"Okay." Is the only word I can manage, and Cash pulls me in to let me know that everything is going to be all right. He inhales a deep breath like he's trying to ingrain this moment. Then, as if they are watching from a distance, Dad and the officer return.

"Miss Rice, have you decided what you would like to do?"

"Yes, sir. I want to file second-degree rape charges and a restraining order."

Without thinking twice, the officer takes the previous paperwork, pushes it to the side, and then pulls up new documents on his desktop and begins to type. Once the items are complete, he gives me a little debriefing about how things will go from here.

"Miss Rice, now that this is in the system, a warrant for his arrest will be made. He will have to appear before the magistrate to see if bond can be made along with the terms and conditions of his release and a court date will be established."

"What do you mean by 'release'?"

"Basically, the magistrate can determine if he can be released with certain regulations. Regardless, he will not be able to come near you."

I shake my head in understanding. The officer leaves to make copies and gives them to me, but not before having a final word with Cash. "Son, if I were you, I'd get myself a lawyer right now. You're gonna need one, but I'll see what I can do. You better pray you get Judge Reeves on the stand. She's as good as they come. She knows her stuff and a good guy when she sees one."

"Yes, sir," Cash says as we stand. We all shake the officer's hand and make our way out of the office to front of the station.

As we open the wooden door, our eyes meet Mr. Sloan. *Oh, shit!* My heart begins to pound, my breathing increases, and I think I might pass out. I try to walk backward, but Cash stops me.

Mr. Sloan looks in our direction with rage engulfing his face. He approaches us swiftly, stopping within inches of Cash. He begins to yell at Cash, pointing his finger and attempting to grab his shirt when the officer approaches and reminds him that might not be the best decision.

Mr. Sloan turns to the officer and informs him that he might want to get to the Grassy Pond Medical Center because his son is fighting for his life thanks to Cash.

"Excuse me, Mr. Sloan. I believe you better not touch him, or you will have charges filed against you. There are some things you don't know about your son, and I'll be more than happy to escort you to GPMC."

With that comment, Mr. Sloan takes a step back from Cash. He and the officer leave through the glass doors while we stand there. As if time has just stood still, we are brought back to reality by the receptionist.

"Yeah, we are fine. Thank you for your help," Dad says as he guides us to the door.

Chapter 6

The ride back to the farm is anything but quiet. I'm actually at a loss for words and in shock from running into Dylan's dad at the station. Dad and Cash, on the other hand, spend the ride talking about the best lawyers in town for and him and me.

As we approach the house, I can see that the lights are still on, and I can only assume that everyone is still awake. The one thing that is different is the extra vehicle in the driveway. Cash's parents are here. Turning, I glance to Cash, and he shrugs his shoulders.

"Cash, I see your parents decided to come over. I think that we all need to sit down and talk about this because I can only imagine what the morning will be like once the Sloans talk to the police tonight."

"Yes, sir," Cash says.

Once the truck is parked, Dad turns off the ignition. "I'm going inside, but y'all take a minute before you come in." We agree with a silent nod. Dad gets out of the truck and makes his way to the house. Mama greets him at the door with a look of sheer panic when we aren't with him. After Dad motions to the truck, she looks relieved, and they go back inside.

I crawl over the front seat and into the back with Cash. His hardworking arms are waiting for me.

We don't talk; we just hold each other. Tears begin to fall from my eyes.

"Char-coal, it's gonna be okay. I promise."

"How can you promise? We don't know what the future holds. I can't live without you."

Removing his arm from my shoulder, he turns to face me. "If there is one thing I'm sure about in the future, it's us. Nothing else matters, Charley Anne Rice. We are going to be together forever. So what if I have to pay the price for taking up for you. I don't care. It will be well worth the time I might have to spend in the big house because I know that you'll be waiting for me when I get out."

"Please don't talk like that. I can't even stand the thought of you in stripes," I say with a half-grin.

At that moment, Cash does what he does. He makes me feel happy inside and out. He starts singing in his most girlie soprano voice. "I hate stripes and orange ain't my color. And if I squeeze that trigger tonight, I'll be wearing one or the other."

Wiping my tears, I begin to grin from ear to ear. Shaking my head, I say, "I can't believe you're singing Brandy Clark's "Stripes." You do know that's about why you don't want to go to jail."

Shrugging his shoulders, he responds, "I know, but I couldn't resist seeing you smile. Come here," he says as he brings his lips to mine.

Right then, I fall even more in love with this boy. He has had my heart for as long as I can remember. He's the other half that makes me whole, and I'm glad that the entire world knows.

Cash gets serious. He takes my hands in his as I face him. I'm not sure that I'm going to like what he's about to say, but I know it will be what I need to hear.

"Char-coal, I think we need to get in there. My parents are probably outta their head about now. Just know that I love you."

"I love you too, Cash Money." I kiss him slowly because I want to savor every moment I have with him.

Cash helps me out of the truck, and we walk hand in hand to my house. As we open the front door, we overhear our parents talking, but before we can even make our way to the kitchen, we are bombarded by the Kluft girls, Tessa, Piper, and Joe.

Tessa is the first one out of the gate with twenty questions. "What happened? Is he gonna get it? They aren't going to do anything to Cash, are they?"

When she takes a breath, I jump in. "Tess, y'all, chill out. It's a lot to explain, but you sending me that text is gonna help put Dylan behind bars for a long time. The only problem is that it's evidence against Cash, too."

They all look at each other and turn as pale as ghosts. "What do you mean?" Piper asks.

"Basically, that video shows Cash beating the shit outta him, and that means he's gonna face charges if Dylan is the typical ass he is... we know he's not gonna let Cash get away with it."

"Well, that just sucks," Hayden says. She's always keeping it real.

"Yeah, it does," I say.

Cash pipes in right after me, "It's one of those things that you hate to have to do, but you know it needs to be done. If I have to do a little time or get a little dirt on my record, I'm okay with that. It's not like I have to pass a background check to work on the farm. Now, if y'all will excuse us, we have to talk to our parents."

Cash and I make our way into the kitchen, and as soon as Cash's mama sees him, she bursts into tears and pulls him into her arms. His dad is standing there with a questioning look aimed at me. Mr. Montgomery has always liked me, but I think he knows that I'm the one that has total control over his son. Needless to say, I don't think he likes that part very much.

Cash gets his mama to calm down, and we all sit at the kitchen table. Dad starts by telling Cash's parents that they need to listen to everything before they ask questions. He tells them that's what they did, and it paid off.

Shaking their head in agreement, they turn their attention to Cash and me. Cash takes my hand and laces his fingers with mine, prompting me to speak.

"Mr. and Mrs. Montgomery, I'm sorry that Cash has been involved in all of this. I want to start from the beginning, but I'm not going to tell you all the details. I've already told this twice, and I really don't want to relive it again. Cash is free to tell you as much or as little as he wants once y'all go home. Also, please wait until I finish to ask any questions."

"Charley, I believe we can do that, but you have to understand that Cash is our child, and we will stick with him no matter what. The fact that there seems to be so many secrets is what bothers me the most," his dad says.

"I understand that." Taking a deep breath, I tell them the nightmare that began a year and a half ago. I do leave out as much detail as possible, but when I talk about Christmas break and the plan that I put in place, I see Mrs. Montgomery start to get fidgety. I pause and tell her to hear me out.

Once I get to tonight with the party, police station, box of evidence, and how we all fit in this awful puzzle, Mrs. Montgomery begins to cry just like my mama. It must be a "mama thing" because I believe she understands what has happened, why certain events didn't add up over the time, and now what Cash is going to have to deal with thanks to me.

When I finish, Dad chimes in, "Y'all, I know it's hard to understand, and if I hadn't heard Charley tell this story twice, I'd be in the same boat as you. One thing I want you to know is what Cash did what was right, even though he might have to pay the price. He did what any of us would do for the woman we love. I can't thank him enough. He saved my sweet girl when I couldn't. My best advice is to call a lawyer tonight or in the morning. The Sloans aren't gonna let this one go. That is one thing I'm sure of."

Silence fills the air as we wait for Cash's parents to speak. Instead of waiting, Cash takes matters into his own hands. "Mama and Daddy, I know this is a lot to think about, but I had to. I love Charley, and if you had seen her that night, you wouldn't be able to live with the guilt that I didn't save her from it happening at all. I will say the last month has been the longest of my life. I've known what was going on and had to watch Dylan touch her. Charley is a helluva woman because I'm pretty sure I couldn't have gone through with this plan. But… tonight… I had to take over. He was going to kill her. I know he was, and I couldn't watch that no matter if I never get outta jail."

Mr. Montgomery begins to speak. "Son, one thing I want to say is that I'm proud of you. You know what you want and never give up, but dammit, I don't want to watch my son go to jail. You know the Sloans have a lot of power in this town, and I just don't know how we are going to afford a great lawyer."

Cash's mama turns to him quickly. "Really? You're worried about the cost? This is our Cash! I don't care what it costs, if the farm goes under or anything else, because that is my baby!"

Whoa! I have never heard Cash's mama talk like that to his dad. She is usually pretty quiet, but I guess that's what happens when you start talking about someone's baby, even if he is nineteen.

"Aight, we'll get the best. Cash, just know you are going to have to help even more around the farm."

"Yes, sir," Cash says.

My mama, being the fine woman she is, decides to give her two cents. "Y'all, I think we need to try not to worry about that right now. Maybe we can both worry about lawyers in the morning 'cause Charley is going to need one as well." That thought makes my stomach turn. *A lawyer.*

After spending a few minutes discussing what we will do tomorrow, Cash and I excuse ourselves while our parents talk alone. We make our way to the living room to find everyone else waiting impatiently. We tell them that tomorrow's gonna be a rough one, and tonight we just want to try to take our minds off of it.

"So, what do y'all say we go to Turtle's?" Tessa asks.

"Are you sure that's a good idea? I mean, I don't want attention to be put on us any more than there has to be," I say.

"I guess you're right. What do you say we grab a movie and hang out here then?" Tessa suggests.

I look at Cash, and he smiles. "Sounds good to us, as long as I get to pick," I say.

Everyone looks at me, and then they say in unison, "*Sweet Home Alabama*, we know."

"How'd ya guess?" I smirk.

Chapter 7

We all sit in the living room and watch my favorite movie of all time. As I watch it this time, I can't help but think how glad I am to have Cash beside me as I nestle more into his arms. He wraps his arms tighter around me, and I look up into those wanting eyes. I know that he wants me as much as I want him, and one day I'll be his forever.

As the movie ends, Joe and Piper stand to go back to her house while the Kluft girls and Tessa head upstairs. Cash and I stay in each other's arms.

"I probably need to go home, Charley. I'm sure my parents want to talk to me." I know that he needs to go home, but I can't help but be selfish. I want him to stay with me. If this is the last night I have with him, I'm not sharing. Funny how he said the same thing to me about a month ago.

"Cash, can't you stay? Just call and tell them you'll be home before sunrise."

"You know I can't resist you, don't ya? Let me call 'em real quick." Cash takes out his phone and calls his parents. They aren't happy, but they understand. He sets his alarm for before dawn and then pulls me closer, and I fall asleep in the arms of my knight in a pair of Carhartts and an F250.

We are awakened to the awful sound of his alarm. He tries not to wake me by slowly sliding his arm out from around me. It's so sweet, but I know he doesn't think that I'm going to let him leave without a proper goodbye.

"Mornin,' Cash Money. Not tryin' to sneak out, are ya?"

"Of course not, but I really didn't want to wake you. You know you're beautiful when you sleep. I was really planning on hitting the snooze for five more minutes."

"Sounds good to me." Cash holds me tight for another five minutes before the snooze erupts from his phone. As much as we both don't want to leave each other, we know we have to. Cash has to go home and prepare for what is bound to happen with Dylan. I, on the other hand, have to prepare to talk to a lawyer as well, but I know that the ball is in my court on this one.

I walk Cash to his truck, and we take as much time as we can to prolong the inevitable. "Charcoal, I love you, and it's gonna be fine. Now, go inside and enjoy your friends, and I'll talk to you as soon we get a plan together."

"Okay."

He takes my chin in his hand, and my eyes meet his. "I promise we will have our forever," he says as he takes control and crashes his lips onto mine.

When we separate, my lips tingle from his touch, and I make my way back to the house. Mom, the Kluft girls, Tessa, and Dad are in the kitchen.

We sit and eat Mama's fabulous breakfast as usual, but things are a little quieter than normal.

As we finish, Georgia speaks, "Char, we're going to head back to campus today. We want to stay with you, but we have practice, registration, and we feel like you need to do this with your family. If something changes, we'll be glad to come back. We love you, but we feel like we're in the way."

"Y'all aren't in the way, but I understand what you mean. I'd want to get back to normal, too. I should probably call Coach."

"No need," Tori states. "I already did. She said take your time, and your spot is there when you get back. Oh, she also said that she'd get your registration taken care of, too."

"Thanks, y'all have taken care of it all. I don't even know what to say."

Hayden starts to giggle. "How about you take that mofo down?" We all start to laugh. I just love these girls.

After breakfast, the Kluft girls get ready and pack up to go back to Southern. Tessa and I meet them outside to say our goodbyes. I'm sad, but I understand. There are a few tears shed when they leave, but Tessa is there to help me pull myself together. Never in a million years did I expect to find a group of girls that are this special to me.

Tessa and I go inside to talk to Mama and Dad. While we are discussing which lawyer we need to see, Tessa says that Dustin has talked to the police about Dylan, and he will be arrested as soon as he is out of the hospital. Dad begins to make a call to a former classmate and now lawyer in town, Becky Horn. She's as good as they come, and she can see us right after lunch today.

Glancing out of the window, I notice a patrol car passing my house. I look back at Dad and begin to freak out. I know this is the moment. The moment that will cause my Cash Money to have to pay the price for me. I start to stand, but Dad stops me. There is one problem; I can't.

Jumping up from the table, I run out the side door and head toward the Montgomery's farm. I have to get to him. I can't let this happen. In the middle of all this chaos, I see my world crashing and rebuilding at the same time.

Knowing that I can't make my way to him by foot, I grab my four-wheeler and haul ass to his house. As I approach, I see the officers making their way toward the front porch. They wait, and then Cash answers the door. I pull the throttle more as I urge to get to him. I know I can't save him, but I need to be there for him like he was for me.

As the officers stand and begin to explain the charges and read Cash his Miranda Rights, I close in on the house. Hopping off the four-wheeler, I sprint to Cash as tears begin to fall as I watch them place him in handcuffs. An overwhelming wail comes from within me, "Noooooooo! Please don't take him. I'm begging you!"

As I reach for him, the officers remove my hands, and I crumble toward the ground only to be comforted by my dad. *When did he get here?* I briefly think before continuing to fall to pieces. Knowing that I need to be strong, I pull myself from my self-pity with my dad's help.

Standing, I can see Cash being placed into the back of the cop car, and I begin to slowly make my way toward the car with Dad by my side. I have to tell him I love him if nothing else.

"Officer, can you wait a minute?" I ask between sniffles. He nods.

Walking to the glass, I place my hand on it, and Cash does the same. I look through the glass into his eyes and tell him I love him, and he does the same. Blowing him a kiss, I back away and watch as the car pulls down the driveway. When I can no longer see him, I turn to my dad and bawl my eyes out.

Chapter 8

As I continue to cry, I hear the voice of Mr. Montgomery. They are eager to find out the outcome once Cash comes face-to-face with the magistrate. Wasting no time, they call Cash's lawyer and make their way to the police station.

Dad wraps his arms around my shoulders and hugs me close. He guides me to the truck, leaving my four-wheeler, and we drive in silence back to our house. When we arrive, we don't get out. Instead, Mama and Tessa meet us and get into the truck. It's time to talk to a lawyer about the situation with Dylan. The sooner this is over, the better.

There aren't but two sets of attorneys within Grassy Pond. As we arrive at the small brick building, I notice the place looks pretty well maintained, unlike several of the offices in town. We get out, and Dad tells the receptionist that we are here to see Becky Horn. She picks up the phone, and we take a seat for what feels like an eternity. Finally, we are called back to Mrs. Horn's office.

Walking into the office is very intimidating. There is fine furniture around, perfectly placed books, chairs, and the smell of dominance permeates the air. I think I like her already. I know someone strong is going to have to be up for this battle, and Becky Horn is it.

We take our seats around the long table as she takes out my file. Without saying a word, she reads it quietly and then removes her reading glasses. She places her hands in her lap and begins to speak.

"Miss Rice, I'm Becky Horn. I'm glad to meet you, but not under the current circumstances. I'm sure you do not want to hear this from me, but before you got here, I was on the phone with the district attorney. We will be working together on the case. He informed me that Mr. Sloan has been arrested as well. He's getting booked as we speak." Panic fills my eyes as I look at Tessa. She knows what I'm thinking. Cash is getting booked, too. Now, if that ain't some shit, I don't know what is. As if she can read what I'm thinking, she continues, "They aren't going to be near each other if that is what you are worried about, sweetheart. That has been made sure of already."

Relief washes over me, and I'm able to actually listen to what she has to say. "Charley, I wish you would have come to the police about this sooner, but I do understand why you didn't. These four walls are completely confidential. You need to tell me everything that you can and not hold back any information. I know that we have solid evidence, but the Sloans have big money and are going to do what they can to make you look like the bad guy. No matter what, we are coming out on top. So, are you ready for this?"

"Yes, ma'am," I answer.

Mrs. Horn informs us of everything that will happen once Dylan goes before the magistrate. She believes the judge will not go lightly on him. Even if he has bond, she thinks it will be high with a lot of restrictions. He will most likely not be able to leave the county. I am able to do pretty much what I like, and she believes that I should return to school and keep things as normal as possible until the hearing. My parents, Tessa, and I agree, but I know I don't want to leave Cash. I ask what might happen to him, and she explains the worst-case scenario. Needless to say, I'm hoping the judge sees that he was defending me.

Once we discuss a few more items, we shake hands and leave. We won't have to do much until the court date is upon us, but that will be like a huge cloud lingering above my head. I don't say much as we get into the car. Tessa takes my hand and just holds it. That's enough right now. Honestly, it's not enough. I need to know what is going on with Dylan and Cash.

Rather than driving back to the house, Dad stops at the general store for a few items for the farm. Tessa and I don't get out. I stare out the window unaware of my surroundings. I'm brought back to reality when Tessa gets a phone call from Dustin.

I wait anxiously for her to hang up. She gets very quiet on the phone, and I'm unsure what type of conversation she's having with him. Uneasiness fills my veins. I know that I will get a few answers, but in my heart of hearts, I'm uncertain if I want to hear them. She hangs up, and I give her no time to process her conversation with him.

"What did he say?" I question.

She looks at me, and tears form in her eyes. "He said that he can't see me right now."

"He what?" I ask as I snap my head toward her. "What the hell? It's not your fault." Realizing I need to push my emotional roller coaster to the side, I know it's time to let Tessa lean on me. I slide close to her and let her cry. "Ya know, maybe it's his parents. You know he loves you, and y'all are perfect together. Just let this pass and see what happens." She nods, but the tears continue to stream down her face. I don't bother asking about Dylan or Cash, because right now, my sister is what is important.

Mama and Dad are taking their time, and I'm glad. Tessa begins to brush away the tears. "I know that's why; he's doing what makes them happy. He used to tell me all the time he wished he wasn't a Sloan. Hopefully, once this is over, things will be okay, but you have to know what else he told me."

"You don't have to, ya know."

"Yes, I do. He said that they just got the verdict from the magistrate." I listen carefully. "You want the good or bad news first?"

"Bad, I guess."

"Dylan is being held on a $95,000 bond with a court date in a month. He can't leave the county, though, so he can kiss his college career and swimming career goodbye."

"Okay, but $95,000 is nothing to his family. I'd be surprised if he's not on his way out already. So, what's the good news?"

"They ran into Cash's family because he was next in line. They hung out long enough to see what was going to happen to him. He got a $7,500 bond until his court date in a month because they have their own lawyers."

"That's awesome."

"What do we do now, Char?"

"Well, it's like this. We stick together because we always have and always will. You were my best friend before Cash, and I know that we will always be there for each other."

"I love you, Char, even if I don't say it enough."

"You don't have to because I know. I love you too, Tess."

We wait until our parents return to make it back to the farm. I'm dying to hear from Cash or his parents, but I really want to talk to Dustin. I have to know if he's pushing Tessa to the side because of his family. If so, I have to tell him to fight for her because she's not worth losing.

Chapter 9

Once we are home, all of us try to get back to a normal day. Dad goes to work on the farm, Mama starts figuring out what she is going to cook for supper, and Tessa and I try to keep our minds occupied. Tessa decides that she doesn't want to stay home and goes to her friend Sally's. I'm on pins and needles to hear from Cash, but as soon as Tessa's car is nothing but dust on the road, I try to get a hold of Dustin. Picking up my phone, I call because there is no need to text. I need to hear his voice and know how he feels. Just when I think it's going to go to voicemail, a hesitant voice answers.

"Hello?"

"Dustin, can you talk?" I ask.

"Hold up a sec." I hear him fumbling with something and then hear his mama in the background. He says something to her about having to get something for one of his friends and that he will be right back. Once I hear a door shut, he speaks, "Are you freakin' crazy calling me?"

"No, I'm not crazy, but I believe *you* might be. What the hell? My sister is a total mess! I just need to know one thing. Did you mean it?"

Dustin begins to talk, but then stops. "Things are really bad here right now. I can't be with her, but it's to protect her. I have no idea what would happen if she showed up at my house right now."

"So, you didn't mean it? Can I at least tell her that?"

"Yeah, and tell her I do love her. Give me a few days to see how things are around here. Just let her know as soon as I can see her, I will, but I had to make that look real to my parents. I gotta go."

"Okay, I'll tell her. Oh, and thanks for not being like your brother."

We disconnect, and a wave of relief washes over me. Thank goodness! I have got to let Tessa know. I text her to call me ASAP. She calls within seconds.

"Everything okay?" she questions.

"Better than okay for you, I'd say. I talked to Dustin."

"You did what?!" she yells.

"Bring it down a notch. You might want to hear what I have to say."

"Spill it. We're about to pig out on ice cream and watch a sappy chick flick."

"He still loves you, and he's gonna call you as soon as he can. Tessa, he just said that because he had to make it look real to his parents."

She pauses. "Are you serious?"

"Yeah."

"If it's true, I hope he calls soon, because as much as I love him, I can't wait on him forever."

There it is. The sister I know. She's strong, independent, and not going to let anyone, even the one she loves, hold her back.

"I just wanted you to know." I inhale a deep breath. "I'm waiting to hear from Cash. I hope he doesn't have to stay there long.

"Me either. I'll see you in a little while. Love you."

"Love ya, too." We disconnect, and I go to pacing the floor.

I have no idea how much time has lapsed as I continue to pace, running different scenarios through my brain. My mind begins to run wild when the most beautiful voice begins to speak.

"Slow down there, Char-coal, before you wear the floor out." I freeze. It can't be true. Oh my gosh, but it is. I stop, turn on my heels, and see the most perfect man to ever exist on this Earth.

"Cash…" I manage to utter before he rushes toward me and swoops me up into his arms. We don't use words; we use actions to show our emotions. I never want to risk losing him again, even though I know that possibility is still in the future. So, until that day, I'm not going anywhere.

Chapter 10

Cash and I spend the remainder of the day doing what we do best, spending time with each other on the farm. We take rides on the four-wheeler, fish, and attempt to keep our minds off things.

As nighttime approaches, we have a decision to make. Do we go home to our own houses, or do we stay here?

"Cash, you're not leaving me tonight."

"I wasn't planning on it. I do need to go home for a little while. You wanna go?"

I nod in agreement, and we make our way to his house. We have been avoiding the conversation about our future. Instead, we focus on the here and now.

Opening the screen door to Cash's house, we are hit with the wonderful aroma of his mama's cooking. Needless to say, she and my mama are neck and neck with who's the best. I look at him, and he knows what I'm thinking.

"Wanna stay for supper?"

"I think that's obvious, don't you?"

"Yeah, I figured."

Walking in, Cash hollers to let his mama know we are here. We enter the kitchen, and she is drying her hands with a dishtowel. Then, she walks toward me and embraces me in a tight squeeze.

"Charley, I want you to know I don't blame you for anything. No one understands why we're at this point now, but God knows and has a plan. You have always been my Cashy's favorite; therefore, you will always be my favorite. He loves you, and we do, too. We're all in this together."

"Thank you," I reply as she lets me go, and we set the table.

When Mr. Montgomery enters the kitchen, he is taken aback when he sees me. "Charley," he says with a nod before he excuses himself to clean up for supper.

I'm uncertain of how to take that, as Mrs. Montgomery gives me her two cents. "He just has a lot to understand, take in, and figure out. Regardless, he feels the same way that I do about you. He is just dealing with things differently."

When Mr. Montgomery returns, we all fix our plates and eat. Things are quieter than usual, but not uncomfortable. At the table, they discuss what the plan is for the future and possible outcomes for Cash. I don't say much; it's not my place. In fact, I just want to disappear at the moment.

After supper is finished, we help clean up, and then I walk upstairs with Cash to pack a bag and gather a few other essentials for the club.

"Are you sure they're all right?" I ask as I help him stuff a few movies into the bag.

He stops, walks around to my side of the bed, and turns me to face him. Taking my chin in his hand, he tilts my eyes to his. "They're fine. It's a lot to take in. Remember, we are all that matters. When this is over, everything will be exactly like it's supposed to be."

"I just don't know, Cash Money. I feel like this might make things different."

"What do you mean?"

"I feel like after this is over, people aren't going to look at me the same. Do you think people 'round here will believe me?"

He wraps his arms around my body. "I know it's true, and that video proves it to all that weren't there. If they don't believe it, then they're just as bad as him."

We finish getting everything together and go by my house to pick up a few things as well. When we walk inside, Mama has a basket packed.

"What's this?" I ask.

"Sweet girl, I've known y'all long enough. I'll see you in the mornin'," she says with a wink.

After I hurry upstairs to grab a few items, we are on our way. I'm so ready for this, and I know Cash is, too.

Today, we drive his truck out there instead of our ATV's. There is a chill in the air when we reach the club. I pick up the basket while Cash gathers our bags. He goes up first and then takes the basket from me so I can make my way up.

Once we are situated for the night, we take a look inside the basket, and I can't help but smile. PB&J's, Choice Cherry Gold, and Mama's homemade peach cobbler. I laugh when I look at what else she put in there. A bag of popped popcorn with M&M's.

"What's so funny?"

"Mama. She knows us too well." He smiles when I pull it from the basket.

"Yes, she does."

Cash takes a blanket and lays it on the floor while I move the basket beside us. I stand after I place it on the floor, and I'm met by warm, rough, yet tender, hands reaching under the hem of my shirt. Cash wraps his arms around me from the back, and I turn my neck to meet him. As I do, he places a tender kiss on my neck.

"I wouldn't do that if I were you."

With a smirk, he replies, "Why's that?"

"'Cause stuff like that can lead to trouble."

"After the past forty-eight hours, I'm up for a little trouble."

"'Bout damn time," I say as I turn to face him and take charge.

For the first time in a long time, Cash lets me take the lead. My lips press his firmly and forcefully. The hunger I feel for him has only increased with our current situation. I'm not willing to put off showing him how I feel.

Unable to control himself any longer, he lifts me off the ground, and I wrap my legs around his firm body. It's very evident how much he is enjoying this. He takes me to the futon and lays me down as he hovers on top of me. *This is it!* We continue to explore each other's body, and when I go for his belt, he stops. *OMG! He's killin' me here!* He shakes his head no. Looking into those beautiful eyes, I give him the saddest face possible and try to work my magic.

Cash places his hands on each side of my head as he looks directly into my puppy dog eyes. "Char-coal, I've already told you about that."

"Can't we just mess around or somethin'? You're killin' me!" I exclaim.

"We could, but not right now. I don't want our emotions to be the reason things happen. If I know you, you're thinkin' about a million what ifs in that cute mind of yours." I can't say anything because he's right. He bends down to my lips and kisses them quickly. "That's what I thought. Come on," he says as he stands and pulls me up.

Crossing my arms and pouting my lip, I respond, "You're no fun."

"Oh, Char-coal, I'm too much fun. You might not be able to handle all of this."

"How about let's just see about that?" I smirk.

"We will one day ... *soon*," he says with emphasis.

Soon? What does that mean? Is he already planning this out in his mind? I start to get giddy inside.

"Slow down, Char-coal. I see those wheels spinning. You're never gonna know when it's gonna happen, but I promise you, it will be sooner rather than later," he says as he steps closer to me. "One thing I've realized is that I'm not takin' anything for granted. Life is precious; you are precious, and our forever is gonna be sooner rather than later."

As his hand grazes my cheekbone, I get weak in the knees. "I can't wait until our forever is really forever."

"Me either." He seals the deal with a kiss. "Now, let's eat. Whatcha say?"

"Well, I guess since you aren't gonna let me have what I want…" I say with a wink.

He grins and takes me by the hand, and we sit on the blanket and enjoy our picnic basket full of goodies that Mama has prepared. While we eat, we talk, laugh, and dream. No matter what is going on around us, when we are inside the club, we are in our own world.

We clean up our trash and go down to the pond. Cash places his hand in mine, and we walk around. The sound of nature is peaceful, and it allows us both to think about what is really on our minds.

"Cash Money, what do you think the judge is going to decide… for you, I mean?"

"It can go two ways, an easy way out or serving some time. Char-coal, it was a felony to do what I did. If I wouldn't have put him in the hospital, I'd have been a lot better off."

"What did your lawyer say?"

"He felt like since I have a clean record and I was trying to protect you, the judge will take that into account. He said I better be ready to get ripped to shreds on the stand, though."

"Yeah, I got told the same thing. It amazes me that even though we aren't guilty, we're going to have to go through hell and back to deal with this. I'm so sorry I waited, but I just couldn't go to the police back then."

Cash stops walking. "Char-coal, you want my real opinion?" I shake my head yes as he replies. "I'm glad it happened this way. I believe this is how it was supposed to happen. Imagine if it was just you and me against Dylan? How do you think that would have turned out? Now, the world knows. Charley, you made him famous in this small town in a way that he never wanted. Every girl that might have come in contact with him should be grateful."

We finish our walk around the pond and then make our way back to the club. Cash pours the movies out onto the floor and lets me choose. "You know what I want to watch, but why don't we watch something different? What about *Ghost Rider*?"

"I mean, if that's what you want. I'm not gonna complain about watching a non-chick flick."

"That's what I thought."

Cash takes the DVD and gets it ready while I grab our drinks and M&M popcorn. We find our spots side by side on the futon. The spot where I fit perfectly in his arm. As I let my head rest on his shoulder, he kisses my hair, and we enjoy the remainder of our night in each other's arms.

When we wake up the next morning, I know it's time to return home. I have a major decision to make today. Do I return to Southern, or do I not? I love it, but I love Cash more.

"Whatcha thinkin' 'bout?" Cash questions as he moves my hair from my shoulder.

"You don't want to know."

"Why wouldn't I? I need to know everything you're thinkin', even though most of the time I already know. Let me see if I can guess."

"What, are you a damn mind reader?" I sass.

"Might be. How about if I get it right, then whatever is racing through your mind, I get to decide the outcome?" This makes me beyond nervous. Cash can read me like a book, but honestly, I need him to decide, because I'm not sure if I can.

"Aight. Shoot. Whatcha think I'm thinkin'?"

Scratching his chin like he's deep in thought trying to decipher my thoughts, Cash says, "If I was a mind reader, I'd say you're debating about going back to Southern."

Speechless. Yeah, that's what I am. My face must tell it all because Cash doesn't give me any time to respond. "The answer to that verdict is… you're goin' back."

"But…" I start to say, but he doesn't allow me to finish. Instead, he covers my lips with his finger. "Shhhhh… just hear me out." Knowing I don't have a choice, I listen. "I know you're scared. I am too, but you went to Southern for a reason. You're

67

not a quitter, and I won't allow you to not finish this year. You have too many people that need you there. The Kluft girls, the team, and Joe."

"But, what if they put you away, and this month is all we have?"

"What did I tell ya about the what ifs? God knows the future, and I believe that He's on our side. He's gonna take care of us. We are meant to be, but you have grown so much these past few months, I can only imagine what you will be like when this year is over."

As tears form in my eyes and one trickles down my face, Cash wipes it away. "Charley Anne Rice, you have grown into a stubborn, fierce, and loving woman that I plan on making my wife one day. You always say I'm your rock and that I saved you, but you save me every day. I'd just be another good ol' country boy, but with you... I'm the good ol' country boy with the strongest country girl by his side, and I'll take that any day."

I don't want to agree, but I know I have to. He's right; he always is. Cash and I hold each other, and by mid-morning, we know we have to go back home. We pack our things and load his truck and drive it through the field to the house.

Dad gives us a wave as he drives the tractor. Tessa's car is home, and I'm sure Mama has a few leftovers from breakfast for us.

Once we are at the house, Cash turns off the truck and looks at me. "So, when are you going to return to Southern?"

Taking a deep breath, I reply, "I guess the sooner the better. Southern States is in two weeks."

"I've got to go home after we eat and talk to Mama and Dad. Then, I'll come back and help you pack." Tears begin to stream, and a wave of emotions hit me even though I try to force it back. I don't want to leave, but I need to do this. Just like the day I decided to go to Southern. I just know. Cash wraps his arm around my shoulder and pulls me in tight, and when I glance at him, his eyes are glossy and tears begin to slide down his face one at a time. Not knowing what to do, I turn to face him, and press my lips to his. We both continue to cry as our lips ignite. In this moment, we have both started to heal with each other.

Chapter 11

We pull ourselves apart, and wipe away each other's tears before exiting the truck. Cash takes my bag, and we walk hand in hand into the house. For some reason today, I feel like it's a new beginning.

Cash lays my bag by the door, even though my mama can't stand that because we used to do it all the time. We go into the kitchen where two plates are fixed and resting on top of the stove. I nuke them in the microwave as Cash pours us some drinks.

We hear Mama in the laundry room. "'Bout time y'all decided to show up. Whatcha got planned today?"

Cash peers at me with the *you better tell her look*. "Um, I guess I'm gonna go back to school." She drops the lid on the washing machine and flies into the kitchen.

"You're going today?" I shake my head yes as the tears begin to fall. She rushes to my side and holds me like only a mother can. "You know you don't have to, right?"

"Yes, ma'am, but I need to. I need to finish what I started."

Brushing her hands through my hair, she takes a minute to speak. "There's my girl. I'm going to let your dad and sister know. Whatcha want for lunch before you go?"

"Doesn't matter." With that, she squeezes me tight and then releases me to find them.

I go to meet Cash, and we eat our breakfast. Afterward, he leaves me to go home to see his parents. I don't walk him to the truck because I might not let him go. Instead, I go upstairs to get ready, talk to Tessa, and start packing.

Within the hour, I'm greeted by a light knock on my door. As it opens, I see Cash Money freshly showered and grinning from ear to ear.

"Whatcha smilin' for?" I ask.

"Well, the fact that I'm lookin' at the most beautiful girl in the world is a given, but Dad talked to my lawyer, and things are looking good. I mean, we haven't been to court yet, but he thinks it's gonna be okay."

Tossing the shirt I was folding onto the bed, I walk toward him and wrap my arms around his neck. "Now, that's the kinda news I like to hear."

He kisses me quickly. "Yeah, me too." We stare into each other's eyes until I feel like I might burst into flames. "C'mon. Let me help ya," he says with a playful smack on my ass.

Cash helps me pack, making me laugh in the process. We take turns stealing kisses from each

71

other, and once things are ready to go, he takes me in his arms, holds me like our lives depend on it, and kisses me with every ounce of his being.

"Um… I guess I need to call Piper. Things have been so crazy."

"She's gonna kill ya for not letting her know you were leaving the moment you decided."

"I know. Joe was going back this morning. I didn't really want to interrupt that love fest."

"I will have to say, I'm glad to see them both happy."

"Me, too. Hold that thought while I call her."

Cash does exactly that. He puts his thought in action as I'm trying to keep a straight face while talking to Piper. I give him the look as he continues to place small kisses on my neck. He grins, but continues. Piper isn't happy that I waited, but understands it was last minute. She's decided that she might as well leave today, too.

We hang up, and I scold Cash, but in a way he really likes.

"You are too cute when you are tryin' to be serious, ya know? It's pretty hot actually."

This only makes me madder, but it doesn't take long before I'm not mad and falling even more in love with the boy of my dreams.

Cash takes the bag downstairs, and Mama is busy finishing lunch. It's simple today, a grilled cheese sandwich and homemade vegetable soup. We all eat as a family, Cash included. Then, Cash and Dad put my bags into the car while I spend a few minutes with Mama and Tessa.

While Mama is moving the clothes to the dryer, Tessa and I talk about Dustin. She's all right now that she knows it's an act. I love my sister more than life itself, and I'm glad that she's going to be fine.

Once the car is loaded, I say my goodbyes to everyone. Poor Blue looks as sad as the first time I left Grassy Pond, so I reassure him I'll be home soon. It's the truth; the court date will be on us quickly. I hug everyone, and Cash walks me to my car while everyone else retreats inside.

Cash pulls me in close; I want to be as close to him as possible. He kisses my forehead down to my lips, and we allow our mouths to do the talking instead of our voices.

Cash's hands roam to the back of my neck and hold me close, as if he can't get enough. He slows, but continues to give me small kisses, and then pulls away. He kisses the tip of my nose before he opens the door. I get into the driver's seat. He kisses me again and tells me he loves me before closing the door. It takes every ounce of courage to crank the car and pull out of the driveway. I know that it's the right choice, even though I'm leaving my heart in Grassy Pond.

Chapter 12

Looking into the rearview mirror, I see the house get smaller and smaller as I drive down the gravel road. Cash is standing there waving bye, and I smile as my heart hurts to leave him.

As I approach the only stoplight in Grassy Pond, I mess with the radio. I'm brought back to reality when I hear a loud truck engine and horn honk beside me. Looking to my right, I smile and can't believe my eyes.

Rolling down my window, I ask Cash Money what the hell he's up to.

"Hey, Char-coal, meet me at the county line gas station."

"Aight," I say as the light turns green, and I take off.

As I reach the county line, I pull off into the gas station parking lot on the right. After turning off the ignition, I reach for the door when it opens for me.

"Well, ain't that sweet," I say as I kiss his cheek once I'm out of the car. "What's all this about? Didn't I just leave you a few minutes ago?"

"Exactly," Cash says as he pulls me against his taut chest. "I couldn't let you go quite yet. I need you to myself for just a few minutes."

"Oh, really? Sayin' bye in front of my parents wasn't good enough for ya?"

"Hell no, and to be honest, I don't know how I'm gonna make it until Southern States."

"Well, then don't! Follow me back now."

Looking at me quizzically, he replies, "Charcoal, I can't go back to school with you."

Knowing exactly what to do, I make Cash think twice about what I just proposed. Taking my hands, I place them on his chest and venture them north until they are around his neck. Using my eyes to tell him everything I'm thinking, I move myself closer to him, and when I'm within inches, I propose the question again. "Are you sure you don't wanna follow me?"

"Char-coal, there would be no followin' you because there's no way I could drive to Southern knowing you're in the car in front of me."

Bringing my lips to his, I kiss him gently, and between kisses, I tell him what he wants to hear. "Why don't you drive me then?"

"Char, where are we gonna leave your car?" he questions as he rests his head on my forehead.

"We take it home, get you some clothes, and hit the road."

"I can't move into your dorm room. This ain't a buy one education get one for free deal."

Laughing, I say, "I know, but I really don't need my car because we ride in the Love Machine anyways. If I need something, I have Georgia or Joe." Giving him the biggest puppy dog eyes and pouty lip possible, I plead for him to take me back. "It will just be for tonight, and then you can come back home. One more night, Cash Money?"

He runs his hand through his short hair, knowing he can't tell me no. "Let me go home and grab some clothes, but why don't I just drive your car? That way you don't have to move all your stuff," he says as he motions to the bags in the backseat along with a full trunk, thanks to Christmas.

Jumping into his arms, I give him small, quick kisses on those perfect lips. I pause before answering him. "I guess you have a point about the car. I'll meet you at your house."

"This is gonna be fun when I pull into your parents driveway tomorrow."

"Cash, really? They love you. They love me, but they love *us* even more. It's okay."

"I hate to break it to you, Char-coal, but in your dad's eyes, it will never be okay. You're his little girl, and even though he trusts me, that's just a conversation I'm not lookin' forward to." I must have a confused look on my face. "You're serious, aren't you? You don't get it. Look, if I drive you back, your parents will know I stayed in your dorm room alone with you. They will only assume, especially after everything that has happened over the past few weeks." Whispering, he says, "You know they think we've done the deed."

"Ohmygosh, Cash! I bet they think we already have!" A look of fear crosses his face. "Nah, I'm kidding. They know where we are, and what we've decided… or what *you've decided.* They're pretty proud of you for standing your ground with me."

"You talked to them both about it?"

"Well, after everything with Dylan, there are no secrets. I'm an open book for everyone to read. So, are you goin' or what?" I ask, changin' the subject.

"Meet me at my house." Kissing my lips, he backs away, gets into the truck, and we make our way back to the Montgomery farm.

Once we are at Cash's, I text Tessa so she will know what's up. Of course, she calls me sneaky as a fox, and she knew as soon as Cash got into his truck, he wasn't going to let me leave the county without him, even if it was for one night.

Cash makes his way out the front door, and his mama waves at me. He tosses his bag into the back, but not before telling me he's driving. Knowing it's a losing battle, I get out and sway seductively to the passenger side.

As I fasten my seat belt, I can feel his eyes burning through me. Looking up, I'm met by my knight in an F250, or maybe a Honda today. "Charcoal, don't do that again. Not in front of my mama, because next time, I won't be able to control myself."

"Oh, really?" I ask as I move my hand from the seat belt to his leg and slide it slowly upward.

"Char, please be good, or I'll stay home."

Crossing my arms playfully, I smirk. "You're no fun!"

"*Fun*? I'll show you fun in about two hours!"

"Now, that's the Cash Money I like to hear," I say with a wink. Cash just shakes his head, puts the car in reverse, and we drive across town one more time.

Our ride to Southern is full of makin' new memories of us together with no thoughts of Dylan, my past, break, or worrying about my future because I'm sitting with my future right beside me. He's always been right beside me.

As we reach the exit toward Southern, we both look at each other when the radio plays Luke Bryan's, "Crash My Party." Taking his hand in mine, he begins to rub his rough fingers across mine.

When the song vanishes from the speakers, he looks at me. I know what he's thinking, but he doesn't give me a minute to speak.

"Char-coal, I love you with my entire being, I know you see me as your forever and I feel the same, but I want to know. When you think about your future, what do you see besides me?"

Not expecting this in-depth question, I take a moment to ponder. "Cash Money, as long as I have you, nothing else matters, but I know you want to hear my thoughts. When I think about my future, I see Grassy Pond, a precious little boy that looks like his daddy but acts like his mama, and if I'm dreamin' big, I'd still like a shot at the Olympic Trials before I give it up."

"Give it up? Why would you do that?"

"Cash, honey, I can't do this forever. Here's a secret. When an athlete hits a certain age, they aren't spring chickens anymore. Not to say that I wouldn't want to coach at GPAC, I just know swimming isn't going to be my career. I'd really like to take over the farm."

He smiles and looks at me. "Is it bad that I hoped that was your dream? I can't see us anywhere but at the farms. I'm glad you went to Southern. God has a plan for each of us, and that was yours. I didn't understand it to start with, but after everything that's happened, I know that was His plan."

Cash Money knows exactly what to say and when and how to say it. I reach across the console and kiss his cheek. "I love you more than life itself, Cash Money, and I'm glad I had this experience as well. I've made friendships that will last a lifetime and a love that was in the works since we were little."

Before we know it, we are approaching campus. A few cars are back on campus. Grabbing some of the bags, we make our way upstairs.

Caroline is standing in the hallway. "Charley, you aren't leavin', are ya?"

Crinkling my nose up, I have no idea why she would say that. "Huh?"

Pointing to Cash, she says, "Helllooo, you brought backup with ya."

"No, silly! He drove me back. He can't get enough of me, ya know?" I wink.

"Well, make sure you keep the noise down tonight!" As I roll my eyes, we walk into my room.

Chapter 13

Once the car is unloaded and we have spoken to the Kluft girls, we make ourselves at home in my room. Cash takes a seat on my bed, and I snuggle into him. We don't say anything, and we wake to the sound of knocking on my door.

"Come in," I say. "Hey, Georgia! Whatcha up to?"

She totally ignores how comfortable Cash and I are. "Oh, we were thinkin' about going out tonight. Since Hank's is not open, we thought we might try that new bar that just opened in town. I think its called The Board Room."

"That's fine with me, if Cash's good with it," I say as I look at him.

"Whatever you want, Char-coal."

"I take that as a yes, so Charley, let's be ready around seven to grab a bite to eat."

"Sounds good." Georgia leaves, and I relax a little longer in Cash's arms.

Realizing that we probably need to do something besides be laid up on each other, I roll and face him. "I think we need to get ready," I say as I press my lips to his. As I back away, he grabs the loops of my jeans and pulls me back to him. I smile on the inside and outside as we take a few minutes to get lost in each other.

As things begin to heat up, I feel Cash start to pull away. "Cash Money, please don't pull away from me." He takes it upon himself to kiss me with loving force. I know why he let up, but it's not easy on a girl to say the least.

He pushes my hand to the side of my face. "Char-coal, I'd never pull away from you, but I told you before that we're waiting."

"But, it's over with Dylan. It's done."

Cash pushes himself up on one arm. "Charley, it's not over. You know we have to go to court over this. Regardless, I told you I'm waiting for our wedding night."

"Well, damn, I just keep thinkin' one day you're gonna give in to me."

"I will one day, and that one day will involve a wedding dress that I'm gonna be ready to rip to shreds."

"Promise me you won't do that because I'm afraid to even think about the price tag on one of those! How about let's get ready to find something to eat? I heard that place has food, too. Maybe everyone will just want to eat there."

"I'm just along for the ride," he says as gets up and kisses my lips. "Let's go see what the plan is."

He helps me up, and we walk to Tori's room. Everyone is in there as usual.

"'Bout damn time!" Tori exclaims.

"What?" I ask.

"Oh, ya know! Y'all come in, and the next thing we know, you're MIA for hours!" she says with a smirk.

"Whatever, y'all! It's not like that... right, Cash Money?"

"You got that right, Char-coal, but ain't nothin' like holdin' you in my arms."

And the entire room goes "Awe."

Shaking my head, I reply, "So, I was thinkin'..."

"Oh, shit! She's thinkin' again!" Hayden says. I shoot her an *are you kiddin' me* look. "What Charley? The last time you started thinking we ended up seeing Cash and his fine ass beating that mofo to a pulp!"

Swallowing really hard, I try my best not to react, not to let my emotions get in the way. As I start to speak, Cash Money takes control, and I can't thank him enough, or maybe I can later!

"Y'all, Char-coal did what she thought was right. Yeah, it got a little messed up, but anything involving Douchebag Dylan is goin' to be jacked up. I'm just glad we were all there," he says as he places his hand around my waist, and I let my head meet his shoulder.

84

"Anyways!" Anna says. "Let's get our party on! What's the game plan?"

"That's why we came in here. We wanted to see if y'all wanted to make a night there. I heard they have some kick ass shrimp and grits!"

Both Hayden and Anna have a disgusted look on their face. "Hey, don't knock it till ya try it!" I reply. "Y'all wanna be ready to roll around seven?"

"Hell to the yeah! There isn't going to be anything bored there tonight!" Tori exclaims.

Hayden starts to laugh, and we all know where this is going. "I can think of a few things that might be stiff as a board!" We all shake our heads and go our separate ways to get ready.

Once we are back in my room, I stare at my closet. I have no clue what I want to wear. As if he's reading my mind, Cash walks up behind me, grabs a pair of Rock N Roll Cowgirl jeans that are completely worn in all the right places and a one-sleeved coral shirt. He pairs it with my new Ariats.

"Here ya go," he says. "This is what I want to see you in, and I'm all that matters."

Acting like I'm going to take the clothes from him, I go to grab them, but instead, I push him onto my bed. It's time to leave Cash like he's been leaving me. I slowly crawl on top of him and kiss his neck and then give a little nibble on his earlobe. When a low moan escapes his lips, I know I'm on the right track. He goes to place his hands underneath my shirt, and I get chills as his tough hands touch my skin. I realize this might not have been the best idea. I slow my movements, but Cash has other ideas.

With his hands on my skin, he rolls me to where this is now his game… and I like it. We spend the next twenty minutes exploring each other, but never crossing the line. If this is that good, I can only imagine what having him completely will be like.

We realize we need to get ready, but we hold each other for as long as we can. I give him a brief kiss before pulling away to take a quick shower. When I return, Cash is dressed and ready to go. Hot damn. He's standing there in a pair of jeans that hug his ass just right and a worn pearl snap, and I'm instantly rethinking this going out idea.

"See somethin' ya like?"

"Maybe?" I smirk as I walk to my desk, turn on Cole Swindell's new album and start to put on my makeup. Cash begins to sing, and when he's right behind me, he bends down, sweeps my hair to the side, and places one tender kiss on my neck. Every nerve in my body is on alert, and chill bumps react on my skin. "What was that for?"

"Is that answer still maybe?" I shrug my shoulders and grin. "Well, let's just see later."

After I finish getting ready, we load up the Love Machine and make our way to The Board Room.

Our ride to The Board Room is nothing out of the ordinary. Hayden is her crazy self. We laugh and enjoy being back together. We don't talk about what happened that night, and I'm glad. I'm ready for some good food with great friends and dancing with the man of my dreams.

Chapter 14

We arrive downtown on two wheels, giggling, and starting the night off right. What's even better is that there has been little alcohol consumed by anyone, and we are still our crazy selves.

Cash guides me out of the Love Machine and takes my hand as we walk up the street to The Board Room. When we enter, the smell of Southern comfort food tickles my nose. The lighting is dim, and people stare at us as we walk inside.

"Um…y'all, is this place supposed to be fancy or something?" Georgia asks.

"Nah, they just aren't prepared for us. That's all," Hayden states confidently as she makes her way to the hostess.

After waiting for a booth to be cleared, we are taken to a back corner in the restaurant. It's hidden away, but we can still see everything around us. There is a DJ setting up not too far from us, families eating a quiet supper, and several couples on dates.

We each take a moment to look over the menu. They have anything from burgers to filet mignon. I know that shrimp and grits are what I will enjoy tonight, and a ribeye is in Cash's future. The waitress approaches and takes our drink order and brings out a basket of bread. Everyone grabs a piece.

Once our order is taken, we sit back, relax, and enjoy being together. Hayden gives us a play-by-play of her crazy adventures while at home on break. I swear, I'd love to have been a fly on the wall when she was little. I bet she stayed in trouble.

The food arrives, and we dig in. It's fantastic. As we all finish, we sit and watch as families leave, and the young crowd begins to arrive at the bar. By nine, the place is crawling with people. Most are young, but there are a few men and women that undoubtedly are single and looking for a good time.

Knowing that this might be our last night out with the swim season being at its peak, we are going to let loose, and I'm glad that they only guy I'll be dancing with is my Cash Money. When the music begins to play, we try to refrain from being the first ones on the dance floor, but that's a lost cause. As soon as the first beat drops, Hayden is out there acting a fool for the entire bar to see.

"Ya know, I'd never have picked Hayden as one of your friends," Cash whispers.

Laughing, I answer, "I know, but I wouldn't trade her crazy ass for the world!"

About that time, I see someone approaching us. It's Joe. Cash extends his hand, they shake, and he takes a seat with us.

"Hey, Joe. Whatcha up to?" I ask.

"Nothing much. The lacrosse guys just figured we'd go out, and when I saw the Love Machine outside, I knew we were in for a fun night."

"You know us too well! Have you talked to Piper?"

His face turns bright red. "Jackalope Joe! Is there something you're not telling us?"

"I have no idea what you're talking about, but I will have to say that girl is something else… and I'll leave it at that."

Cutting my eyes at Cash, I know exactly what that means. Piper has Joe wrapped, and she's not going to let him loose if she can help it. I can't blame her one bit. He's a good one, and if I didn't have my Cash Money, he would definitely be at the top of my get-to-know list.

"Well, I just wanted to say hey. I'm sure I'll see ya on the dance floor in a little bit."

"Wait! Let's send Piper a pic. You think she's back yet?" We send a funny group shot with a message wishing she was here before Joe goes to hang out with the guys.

After Joe leaves, Cash and I sit and enjoy being together. Little by little the dance floor continues to get packed. Cash and I have had a good time sitting here, but now it's time to shake what my mama gave me. Taking him by the hand, I pull him from the booth, putting a little more emphasis on my hips as we make our way to the dance floor.

As we reach it, I turn around and face him. "You know you're killin' me, right?" he whispers.

"I don't want to kill you, but I might want to make you want me just a little bit more."

"Char-coal, that ain't possible, but I plan on enjoying every minute of it."

Smiling, I look him in the eyes and brush my lips against his. Wrapping my arms around his neck, I sway my hips to the beat of the music, and he follows along. Whoever said white boys can't dance sure haven't seen Cash. He doesn't even need liquid courage. With each song, we become more in tune with each other. Everyone around us has disappeared, and we are now the only people I see. That is until Katy Perry comes through the speakers. I'm brought back to reality with the sound of Hayden and all my friends singing at the top of their lungs, and I have no choice but to join in.

Cash stands at the edge of the dance floor with Joe as they watch. He has a huge grin on his face with his arms crossed, and Joe does the same. It's kinda funny how things worked out. Not only do I have the man of my dreams, but my best friend has hers as well.

When the song ends, we continue to dance like we would at Hank's. Every guy in the room is

91

watching us, and we all enjoy it a little too much. As guys start to approach us to dance, I decide I might need to find Cash Money. That's when I feel hands touch my hips that aren't his. Glancing over my shoulder, I see Tucker, the fine ass baseball player. He smiles. I turn to face him and excuse myself, but he doesn't let go of my hips.

"Tucker, I'm with someone," I say as I point to Cash.

"Oh, well, I just thought since you and Joe are a no, maybe we could pick up from where we left off at Hank's."

"I'm sorry, but if you want someone fun to dance with, both Georgia and Caroline are single and fun."

"Okay, but I just thought we had something."

Tucker and I are not going to have anything going, so I separate myself from him and lead him toward Georgia who is talking to Cash.

"Georgia, this is Tucker. He plays baseball and wants to dance," I say confidently.

Georgia looks at me like I've lost it, but smiles and agrees. Tucker introduces himself to Cash and informs him that he is one lucky guy to have me. Cash agrees completely, and they make their way to the dance floor.

Cash places his arm around my waist. "I'm not even gonna ask about that one, but I was about two seconds away from getting my ass put back in jail."

"Now, Cash Money, we can't have that," I say as I turn into his chest, place my hand on his cheek, and make him forget that another guy just tried to make a move on me.

We spend the remainder of the night in each other's arms both on and off the dance floor. When the house lights come up, we make our way to the Love Machine and back to Southern. The ride is full of chatter about Georgia and Tucker and what is going to become of that. He seems like a decent guy, but only time will tell, because those baseball guys have a reputation of taking one thing and leaving. If that's the case, he won't call Georgia again because she's not that kinda girl.

We say goodbye to everyone and wait while they make their way back to their rooms. I have to make sure our residential assistant isn't on the prowl. She's not, so we walk to my room. Once we are inside, we get ready for bed. Exhausted from a night out, I can't wait to fall asleep in Cash's arms, which is exactly what I do, even though I don't want morning to come. In the morning, Cash will have to go back to Grassy Pond, I'll have practice, and we will be apart until his court date.

Chapter 15

I awake to the sound of a bird chirping and the warmth of Cash's arms around me. I don't want to move because that would risk the chance of him stirring, and then he will have to go. Glancing at the clock, I see that it's eight. I have practice at ten. I decide the best choice to make right now is to lie in Cash's arms until I'm forced to get up.

Undoubtedly, Cash is exhausted because I finally have to wake him at nine-fifteen. It's earlier than I want, but I do want to enjoy his company a little bit before he has to leave and I have practice.

As I roll to wake him with a kiss, he smiles at me. "Well, if I didn't know better, I'd think you were just acting like you were sleepin'," I say before meeting my lips with his.

"I'll never tell," he says with a wink as he places his arms around my body. "I really don't want to leave."

"I know. You sure this is the right choice?"

Sweeping my hair out of my face, I reply, "I know it's the right choice. This semester will be over before we know it. Then, I will be home until next year."

Not really wanting to touch the next year subject, I just do what any girl would do lying with the hottest country boy around. I take advantage.

Until we have to get ready, Cash and I have fun in the sheets, but don't cross the line. I'm dreading this moment. It was terrible to leave him in Grassy Pond, and here I am replaying this scene again. He must sense my sadness, as we get ready, because he wraps his loving arms around me as I attempt to pull my hair into a ponytail.

"I don't want to leave either, but I have to. I'm sure your dad would love to have to pay double tuition."

"You're right about that." I smirk. "I could just see his face if he got that kinda bill."

Once I finish putting up my hair, we hold each other until we don't have any other choice but to go our separate ways.

"Come on. Let me drive you to practice," Cash says as he grabs my swim bag and his duffle bag.

Cash gets my keys, and we make our way to my car. He opens the passenger seat for me and kisses my lips before closing the door and walking around to the driver's seat. After glancing at him in the driver's seat, I smirk. *The things a guy will do for his girl, like drive her car.*

"What's that for?" he asks.

"You just look so cute drivin' the Honda."

"Hey, it takes a real man to drive one, but I feel like I'm on the dirt compared to the truck."

95

After placing the car in reverse, he puts his hand on my leg and drives me to practice. As we see the gym approaching, tears begin to swell in my eyes. I try to brush them without Cash noticing, but it's a lost cause.

As we pull into a parking space, Cash puts the car in park and comes to open the door for me. He guides me out of the car by my hand, and I stand as he pulls me in for a sweet embrace. He wipes the tears that are now freely falling from my eyes and pulls up my chin to meet his gaze.

"Char-coal, don't cry. It only makes it harder for both of us. I'm going to try to come back next weekend or at least for Southern States. Maybe Tessa can bring your car, and I'll follow her in the truck. That way you can come home when you want. Know that whether I'm here with you or at home, you are always my first thought. The first one in the morning, constantly during the day, and the last one before I meet you in my dreams."

"I love you, Cash Money, with my whole heart, and it hurts so much to know we have to be apart."

"I love you more, but think of it more as an adventure. While I'm at home in Grassy Pond, you're living the college life for both of us. Not that I regret not going away, but it wasn't my dream… it was yours."

Knowing that Cash is right, I hold him tighter. He brings my lips to his and kisses them sweetly and hugs me again before making me head to practice before I'm late.

"I'll text ya when I'm home. Now, go before you're late. Love you!"

"Love you, too," I say as I turn and walk into the gym, strutting just a little to leave him with a view to remember. That thought makes me smile instead of wanting to cry, so that's what I do. I smile.

Practice is just practice. It's great to be back with Coach and the team. It feels amazing to be back in the pool, especially considering that I didn't get to the pool like I wanted to the last few days. When practice is over, Coach asks to see me.

"Whatcha need, Coach?"

"Charley, come in and have a seat." *This cannot be good*, I think to myself as I take a seat. "I know you probably don't want to talk about it, but I need to know exactly what is going on at home. Word travels fast, and the fact that one of the state's best swimmers has been charged with rape, I just need to know how I can support you."

"Coach, I just want him to pay. I want to stop him from hurting anyone else, and I want to stop looking over my shoulder all the time."

Coach fidgets with a few papers on her desk before she speaks. "Charley, I hope he rots in hell, because I don't care if he is God's gift to the swimming sport, that is unacceptable. The only thing I'm worried about is Southern States. There will be a lot of coverage there, and you are already in the spotlight with your times. Add this story to it, and who knows what will happen? I just need you to promise me that no matter what they say or do, you will keep you head held high and remember we are here for you."

"Yes, ma'am."

"Oh, and Charley, you looked fabulous in the water today. You're gonna leave them speechless."

As I'm leaving Coach's office, I'm met by Georgia and Tori who are dying to know what has gone on. I fill them in fast, and Tori is quick to say that she will take care of anyone that tries to start anything at Southern States. I don't want any more trouble, so I inform her that we are classy Southern girls and will do what any country girl would do. That means put on a pretty face and kick their ass in the water. She loves that idea, and we walk back to Kluft and get ready for our first day of a new semester.

Chapter 16

Cash made it home all right and informed me that he and Tessa will bring back my car next weekend at Southern States. He also told me that I might want to call Tessa because she seemed a little too happy when he saw her. That can only mean one thing; Dustin finally got in touch with her, and I'm beyond happy for her.

Giving a little time lapse between now and calling Tessa, I take a quick shower, glance at my class schedule, and relax. Afterward, I call her. Of course, she answers right before it goes to voicemail.

"Hey, Sis! Whatcha doin'?" she says very perky.

"Um…well, a little birdy told me you were in a very good mood, and I just wanted to see the reason behind it."

"Charley Anne Rice! Do I have to have a reason to be in a fabulous make-your-heart-wanna-melt mood?"

"No, but I know you well enough to know that something has happened. Either you got outta doing chores for the rest of the year or Dustin has made your day."

"Gah, why do you always think that it has something to do with getting' outta work? But, you are right! He called!" she squeals. In all my years,

I've never seen Tessa like this, and I hope and pray that Dustin is her forever like Cash is mine. I know it will make for interesting family functions in the future, but with love, anything's possible.

"What did he say?"

"He said that now that his parents have had time to cool off, they can't stop him from seeing me. They did ask if we would keep it low key until after the court stuff, but regardless, they aren't goin' to stop us from being together."

My heart leaps out of my chest with excitement for Tessa and Dustin. They deserve to be happy despite what has happened between Dylan and me. The fact that Dustin wasn't willing to just let her go makes me love him, too.

"I'm so happy for y'all! Have you seen him yet?"

"Not yet."

"Well, I have an idea. What about if y'all take the club for the night or two? It's not like I'm going to be home to use it, and I know Cash won't care."

"Yeah, let me see what he thinks. Char, thanks for everything. I don't tell ya enough."

"Anytime. Love ya, Tess."

"Love ya, too."

We disconnect, and I text Cash the news as well as Joe and Piper. Come to think of it, I haven't seen Joe much, but I guess it's because he's giving me some space with Cash. As suppertime approaches, the Kluft girls and I make our way to the cafeteria. A million eyes meet mine, and I'm pretty sure that I'm the current talk of the school.

Without missing a beat, we all walk inside with our heads held high, acting like nothing happened over break. I see Joe sitting with his teammates, and he smiles. I'm glad that everything has worked out between us because he truly is a friend for life, and I know that now. Knowing he was willing to risk losing me in order to save me means the world. The fact that he loves Piper just seals the deal with him.

After grabbing a tray, picking out what mystery food I'm going to eat, and taking a seat, I finally breathe. The eyes are no longer on me, but back to everything going on around us. I feel relieved that the initial shock of everyone knowing what happened is over. Word definitely travels fast at a small school. We finish eating and head back to the dorm. Tomorrow's going to be a long day with new classes and practice. We watch TV in Tori's room and then call it a night.

After calling Cash, I fall asleep and dream of our happily ever after only to be awakened by that awful buzz from my alarm clock. Time for practice already? Rolling out of bed, I hear a light knock at the door. Cracking the door open, I see Georgia ready to go. I tell her to give me a second, and we are on our way. Practice is refreshing, and I take my time getting ready for class. Coach was smart enough to give me nine o'clock classes instead of eight. I'll have to thank her later. The day goes quickly, and one or two Kluft girls are in each of my classes. We sit together and make a plan for passing this semester, not that it's going to be a big deal. Once our day is over, we make our way back to Kluft, but I stop to talk to Joe. I feel like I just need to talk to him.

"Hey, Jackalope Joe, you got a minute?"

"Yeah, what's up, Squirrel?"

"Not much. I just wanted to make sure that everything's good. I haven't had much time to talk to you with everything going on. You're important to me... and Piper." The mention of Piper's name makes him smile.

"We're good. Oh, as in you and I or you and Piper?"

"Both. Thank you."

"For what?" I ask.

"For coming into my life. I thought that it would be you and me together, but little did I know that you would lead me to the girl of my dreams," he says with a nudge.

"She is pretty awesome. After me, I mean. You know I'm at the top of the awesomesauce list."

He shakes his head. "So, not to bring up the subject, but when will everything be over?"

"As long as they don't continue it, we should be done within a month or two at the latest. I'm just worried about the verdict."

Joe stares at his feet as we walk. "Yeah, me too."

I stop walking. "Why are you scared? You're in the clear. I've made sure of it."

"I know, but you know they might put me on the stand."

"That is highly unlikely because this has to do with an event that occurred before you were in the picture."

After remaining quiet for a moment, Joe responds, "I guess I know that, but honestly, until it's over I won't be sure."

"Well, as Cash told me, God's got a plan, and we're in it. He will make sure it all works out."

We continue to walk until we are back at Kluft. We make a little small talk before I go upstairs to my room. This has been a pretty good day to a new semester. I'm praying that it's foreshadowing what is to come… only good things.

Chapter 17

The only monumental events that occur between the start of the semester and Southern States are the moments I get to talk to Cash and enjoy my friends. Everything else is routine and like a robot. In fact, I'm excited to see the season end, so that I have a new routine to my day.

We spend the week up to the meet carb loading, practicing, and cramming for any test that we need to take before we leave. I've mentally tried to prepare myself for what could possibly happen when we walk into that aquatic center, but until I'm inside, I won't relax.

We pack our bags and plan to meet Coach at the gym at nine on Friday morning. The drive to Davidson isn't far, but we will need to get there and get our minds right for the meet. Once we are at the gym and loaded up in the Southern van, we make our way toward Davidson. Our ride is full of laughter. Everyone begins to giggle uncontrollably as Coach busts a move when a hip-hop song comes on. We also discuss how we should behave, what happens if someone mentions something about my issues, and how we are going to kick some ass and take names.

As we arrive on the Davidson campus, I'm in awe of how beautiful it is. Even in the end of the winter months, it has the warm look of spring. The buildings are well maintained, and there's a Ben and Jerry's right off campus. I'm glad that isn't the case at Southern because I'd be as big as a house from eating too much Phish Food. Southern is beautiful, but the buildings are worn and need a little TLC. As we pull into the aquatic center parking lot, Coach tells us all to wait before we get out. Unsure of what she might say, we sit there quietly.

"Girls, I'm proud of you no matter what happens. There are some tough competitors here today, but I know that we are just as good. Charley, you're gonna kick ass." We all snicker. "Because you were born for this. You are at home in the water. With the recent events, I know people are watching you. We're on his turf right now. So, everyone needs to be prepared and ready for what might be said. Now, that's out of the way. Let's show them what Southern girls are made of!"

Tori places her hand on my shoulder as reassurance. As we walk toward the double doors, I hold my head high because I am the victim, but I will no longer act as if it controls me. I'm on edge of what might happen, but as soon as we enter, a calmness finds my soul. We bypass the locker room and go straight to the pool. As we approach, the smell of chlorine increases, and moisture and warmth fill the air.

When we enter the pool area, we see several teams already suited up and beginning warm-ups. As we make our way to the stands, eyes begin to focus on us. I turn to my teammates, and we do what we do best. When given the moment to sink or swim, we choose to swim. With a glance in Tori's direction, we know exactly what we need to do… make our presence known.

Silently counting to three, we begin to shout out our Southern cheer, and all eyes focus on the only female only team to enter the arena. Knowing we are getting positive reactions, we let loose. Once we are at our seats, we place our bags on the bleachers and Tori yells, "One, two, three!" And we follow with "Southern!"

Focusing back on the task at hand, we get ready to sit for Coach to let us know when our warm-ups start, but as we wait on her, the team from Howard University is behind us. One of the team members yells, "Hey, Southern girls! Now, that's the way to make an entrance." He winks as he grabs his cap and goggles.

"What can we say? We're the girls from Southern. We always leave our mark with our Southern charm," Georgia states with assurance.

Coach tells us we have twenty minutes until we can hit the water. She also informs us that with the lineup of events we will be here until eight tonight with preliminaries, return to Southern, and arrive back in the morning by eight. *Ohmygosh! Why can't we just get a hotel?* We must all have the same look on our faces.

"Girls, the budget's tight. We need to watch what we spend."

"But, Coach! It's Southern States!"

Tapping her foot, she replies, "Well, let me see what I can do. I think there's a pretty decent, but cheap hotel within a few miles from here."

"Coach, you're the best!" Tori exclaims.

"Well, I try. It's not often that we have a team that can knock a Division One school outta the water. I might need to spoil y'all just a little bit. Oh, do y'all have stuff to stay overnight?"

"Yes!" we reply in unison.

She laughs. "I better call the hubby to contact the hotel and bring me some clothes. Y'all are going to be the death of me! Now, get ready, and I'll see you in fifteen in lanes one and two."

Grabbing our stuff, we make our way to the locker room. We hurry to get ready, and I text my parents and Cash to let them know we are staying overnight. Knowing that Davidson isn't too far from home, I figure they will drive back and return in the morning. I'm shocked when I realize they already have a room booked.

I hear the first whisper as I pick up my bag to exit the locker room. "You know *that's* the girl that got Dylan in trouble." Closing my eyes, I try to force back the tears and control my emotions. They will not get the best of me.

When I walk past them, they stop talking. I stop and look at them and give them a dose of their own medicine. "Yeah, I *am* that girl. Got anything else you wanna know?" I say with my bag tossed over my shoulder and my arms crossed.

"We didn't say anything," one girl states with an eye roll.

"That's what I thought." I make my way back to the stands, placing my bag down and walking toward the pool. Tori and Georgia must see the heat rising in my face because they ask me what the hell just happened as soon as I meet them.

"Some Davidson bitches we're running their traps already. So, I just asked if they had any more questions."

Georgia laughs. "They are so in for it! Charley's gonna kick their ass today in the water."

"Damn right, I am," I say as I dip my cap into the pool, place it on my head and add my goggles. It's time to give them another reason to talk about Charley Anne Rice.

Coach starts us with a five hundred warm-up, and then we complete a few short sets. Once we are loose, we have a team meeting to discuss our events, times, what we hope to accomplish, and the reason we are here. Afterward, we make our way back to the stands and wait.

Grabbing my iPod from my bag, I place my ear buds into my ears and turn up a little Florida Georgia Line and push everything away from my mind. Taking a seat on the bleacher, I lean back, prop myself up, and close my eyes. By song number three, I've forgotten what happened in the locker room…well, maybe not, but I've channeled my feelings. Just as I relax, there's a dip in the bleacher. My eyes shoot open, and that's when I see my four favorite people: Tessa, Cash, Piper, and Joe, along with my parents. A smile spreads from ear to ear, and I remove my ear buds.

"Hey, y'all!" I say as I stand to give them all hugs. I save Cash for last because I want it to last the longest. He kisses my forehead before they leave to find a seat in the fan section.

At exactly noon, we pay respect to our country and God, and the meet is underway. Several individual events occur for our team members, and we are like one driving force pulling them toward victory. When the 200-meter backstroke is five events out, I head to the pool deck to stretch and mentally prepare myself for the event. I look at my family and teammates and am proud of who I am.

When the announcer calls my event, I focus on the water, the number of laps, and what it's going to take to win. That's when I notice that smart-ass girl from the locker room in the lane beside me. This is going to be good. I put on my goggles and wait to be told to enter the water. All I can do is smile at her because I'm about to leave her in my wake.

I enter the water feet first and get ready for the sound of the buzzer. When it fires, I explode off the wall and kick. I continue to make my way toward the end of the pool at a constant speed. The girl beside me is hanging in there with me, but what she doesn't realize is that I'm holding back.

Once we make the turn, I push off the wall and focus on all the bottled-up emotions and take them out in the pool. In my mind, I replay the events in the locker room, what's to come in court, and use that to assault the remaining 150 meters. In doing so, I leave her at least two body lengths behind me.

As my fingers tap the touchpad to stop my time, I feel my adrenaline begin to decrease; yet the excitement within my body begins to rise. Placing the goggles on my forehead, I turn to see everyone approaching. Hurrying to see my time, I look to the display board. *Holy shit!* Not only have I shaved three seconds off my time, but I've also set a new record for Southern.

Pulling myself from the pool, I'm greeted by my teammates. We all embrace, squeal, and jump up and down.

When our celebration is over, I look at the smart ass from the locker room, walk over to her, and tell her good job because I know that will hurt her more than being a bitch like her. Then, I walk with my team back to the stand and am greeted by my own personal fan club.

My parents are extremely proud. Tessa is acting like the Tessa I love dearly, but what I wasn't expecting was for Dustin to be by her side. As I turn to Cash and my parents, fear enters my eyes.

"Charley, you might want to listen to Dustin," Dad says tenderly.

"Listen? More like who brought you? Not that I mind, but I know y'all well enough that there's not going to be a parade of cars going to Southern or Grassy Pond."

"Listen, think, and then speak. Do you understand?" Dad says sternly.

"Yes, sir."

Cash takes my hand in his after I wrap my towel around my body, and we walk toward them. I don't really want to make a scene in front of the other teams, or better yet, watch my team start a brawl. I'm not sure if it is the downfall of the adrenaline or the fact that I know the Sloans are here.

"Charley, before you say anything, yes, my parents brought me and against the better choice of their lawyer. I needed to be here for your family and be with Tessa."

"But why? If they know the lawyers aren't wanting them to, I mean."

"They support me. I'm their son as well. They know that it looks bad for them to have done this, but they also know that I'm a good person. I'm the one that doesn't break the rules or make our lives a livin' hell. That's why."

I don't say anything; instead, I release Cash's hand and engulf Dustin in a hug. At this point, I don't have any words. The fact that his parents brought him to my family is monumental. Not that they are admitting Dylan did anything wrong, but it does show that they care about Dustin and making him happy.

I speak as I pull myself from our hug. "Dustin, when you walked in, I almost freaked. Not because you were here, but because I knew your parents were near. It's just I don't know what they would say to me."

"I can promise you this, Charley. They are surviving, whether you realize it or not. They know Dylan's wrong, but they are still his parents. They are doing the only thing they know how to do… be loving parents through thick and thin."

Dustin is right. I can only imagine what it would be like to be in their position. I know that parents love their children unconditionally regardless of their actions, but I'm sure it's rough.

"Dustin, I'm so sorry that you and Tessa are havin' to deal with all of this."

"Don't be sorry, Charley. He made those choices. It's rough on all of us, but we'll make it. I couldn't live without Tessa in my life," he says as he looks at her.

"You don't have to say anything else. I understand," I say as I guide my fingers into Cash's hand.

Dad looks at Mama. "What?" she asks. "We might need to have a talk with those two girls."

"Honey, I've already done that."

Tessa and I start to laugh. Does Dad really think that we are that naïve? "Dad, we're good. I promise," I say with a little roughness in my tone, and at that point, Cash smirks. *Damn him and his wait until we're married!* To change the subject, we talk about the events and then they make their way back to their seats. All of them know that during this time, I don't socialize… I focus on the task at hand.

Chapter 18

The remainder of the preliminary heats continues without a hitch. As time approaches for our 4x200 IM relay, we mentally prepare for the event to come. We make our way to the pool deck when it is time and begin to loosen up the only way we know how. Stretching in a huddle, we begin to sing Miley Cyrus,' "We Can't Stop," and, of course, all eyes are on us. Near the end of the song, we stand and try to relax our muscles by shaking our arms and legs, and then we head to our lane.

"Hey, y'all. Let's kick some ass Southern style," I say to the girls.

"Hell yeah! Charley, you get us started off right," Georgia says. "Let's see if we can really leave those Davidson girls speechless."

We put our goggles in place and focus on the event. Glancing in the stands, I notice my family, Cash, and other teammates looking in our direction. I have to say the entire conversation with Dustin was beyond weird, but in a way, I'm relieved. I give them a little wave, jump up and down to get a few jitters out of my system and take a few deep breaths as I wait for the announcer to tell us to enter the water. Then, I hear him.

"Swimmers 4x200 Individual Medley Relay. Backstrokers, enter the water feet first." Plunging into the water, I feel my nerves vanish as I grab the start block. "4x200 Individual Medley Relay. Swimmers, take your mark."

There is slight pause before the buzzer sounds. Arching my back as I burst off the wall, I kick with everything that I have. There is no holding back like I did in my individual event. This is for the team, and we are going to leave them all speechless if I can help it. Cutting my arms like blades through the water, I make it to the flags with ease and continue to push myself to beyond my breaking point. On the final lap of my leg of the race, I truly let go of everything that might be holding me back and jet half of a pool length ahead of the others. When my fingertips touch the time pad, Georgia jumps in. Tori pulls me from the water, and I'm cheesing from ear to ear. She points toward the time board. As I look at my leg of the race, chill bumps cover my arms. I have just beaten my own personal record as well as Southern's record, and if all goes as planned, we will be one step closer to Olympic Trials.

Focusing back on the water, we all cheer as our teammates glide through the water, keeping the distance between the other teams. On the last leg, we begin to jump up and down as Sarah brings it home. When she taps the time pad, we all turn straight to see the official time.

We don't say a word; we grab each other and begin to scream like little girls with excitement. *OMG! 9:22:46!* Keeping our composure together, we make our way from the deck and toward the stand. We are still beyond excited. We broke not only our record but also Southern States.

Coach meets us at the entrance to the stands with open arms. She is one proud mama bear of her cubs. "I believe a little Ben & Jerry's is in order. What y'all think?" We hug a few more seconds before going to our seats.

When we get there, the guys from Howard tell us congratulations, give us high fives, and ask if we can join their team. We all cut our eyes and tell them no. One guy looks heartbroken as he places his hand over his heart and pouts. It is beyond adorable. I look at Tori, and she is definitely taking him in. I nudge Georgia, and she laughs.

"I bet she gets his number or meets up with him in the locker room before this day is over. Whatcha think?"

"I'm not taking that bet because we'd be on the same side," I say as someone's arms wrap around me from behind. *Cash.*

Turning around, I hold on to him tightly, hearing a teammate yell for us to get a room in the background. I just turn and grin.

"That was beyond amazing," he says.

"I know, but not as amazing as you. Thank you for *everything.*"

"I know I shouldn't be over here with the teams, so can you come over here for a few?"

"Yeah, just let me let Coach know." I tell her and make my way to my parents, Tessa, and Dustin.

"Ohmygosh, Char! That was freakin' ah-mazing! You kicked ass!" Tessa exclaims.

"Tessa! Watch your mouth!" Mama says.

"Well, it's the truth. Anyways! I wish you could have heard everyone up here. They were all running their mouths beforehand, and then they shut up quick when you left them all behind. If this is just preliminaries, I can't wait to see what y'all do tomorrow."

"I know. I hope we do this well again. We really need those times in the actual events instead of today, but hey, it was worth it, regardless."

"We're so proud of you," Mama says as she pulls me in for a hug and gets soaking wet.

I excuse myself from everyone and go back to my teammates. We take turns going to change as our events come to a close for the night. I shower quickly before returning and watching the final two events.

As the preliminaries come to an end, we gather our things and make our way to the van. Our first stop is Ben and Jerry's. Who needs supper when you can have ice cream?

Chapter 19

We enjoy our ice cream and then check into the
hotel before ordering in pizza. We all pile into one
room for a little fellowship and food. I text Cash
when we finish eating. He lets me know they are in
the hotel half a mile down the road. He says that
Mama and Tessa are in one room and he, Dustin,
and my dad are in another. That should make for an
interesting night. My dad with the two guys that
hold his little girls' hearts. I'd love to be a fly on the
wall tonight. We talk for a few minutes, and I tell
him I'll see him tomorrow. He knows how
important this meet is for all of us. He also knows
that he will hold me in his arms tomorrow night.

I share a room with Tori, Georgia, and Sarah.
We relax, talk about anything and everything, turn
on a movie, and finally fall asleep. We are
exhausted from the adrenaline rush that we have all
felt today.

When the alarm buzzes in the morning, I want
to chunk it across the room. That sound gets worse
and worse each time I hear it. We gather our items
and meet the team downstairs for a continental
breakfast of champs. I devour a boiled egg, bacon,
and a bowl of oatmeal before leaving for Southern
States.

The arena is already beginning to fill with
people in the stands this morning. It is very evident
that today is going to be a lot wilder than yesterday.
We repeat the same events from yesterday, even

down to where we sit. I guess you can say we are all a little superstitious.

After warm-ups, we take our place in the stands and wait until it is time for our events. My family, Cash, and Dustin arrive and give us a wave. Ten minutes later, I see Piper and Joe. It dawns on me that I didn't see them much yesterday, and then I realize that Piper is having her own version of a walk of shame in front of my parents, even though it's not really a shame. She smiles and has a glow about her. *Glow! I know what they did last night! The last time she looked like that was a night she let Justin go a little too far, and she liked it!* Joe says hey to my parents, and he and Cash give each other a welcome and take a seat. Piper looks my direction, and I press my lips together and smirk. I can't wait to talk to her tonight!

Georgia must be reading my mind because she gives her eyebrows a raise, and I giggle. For someone who still has her V card, she sure knows when someone else has done it. I grab my iPod and focus, because today is a day for giving everything I have and more.

The list of events is pretty close to the same as yesterday. Today's meet will fly by due to there only being one to two heats of each event, unlike yesterday, when there were five to six. I wait patiently for the 200-meter backstroke.

When it's time for me to make my way to the pool deck, I am caught completely off guard by

119

several signs being held up in the fan section. They all read *#TeamDylan*. I get sick to my stomach just looking at them. I feel the blood drain from my face, and I hurry to the trashcan to lose all the contents within my stomach. That sick bastard is still trying to scare me. The problem is, I'm not going to let him.

Instead of getting sick, I pull all the fear, anxiety, heartache, and nervousness to my core and walk to stretch with my head held high. What I'm not prepared for is Joe to turn around and yell at those people. I see Cash stand, and all I can think of is him getting in trouble. There is little time to think about what is going on, especially when I see my dad stand and turn as well. He takes a step up the bleachers, and even though I can't understand what he is saying, I know it has to be epic, because after about thirty seconds, they sit. They still hold their sign, but they are quiet, which is what I need to continue to focus on the prize at the end of the race.

As the announcer calls the event, I realize that it is now or never. It's time to make them all stop talking for once and for all. I relax my body and listen for the moment to enter the water. When that happens, it's game on.

Pointing my toes as they enter the water first, I come up and grab the start block. Once the buzzer sounds, I tunnel my thoughts and body toward winning this race, but not against anyone in this pool; I focus on beating myself.

120

With each lap, I dig deeper for more strength to continue to pursue my goal, and by the final lap, I know that if anyone is anywhere near my time it's nothing short of a miracle from the big man upstairs. As the tips of my fingers tap the time pad, I pop my head out of the water and look directly at the time board. Throwing my arm in the air, I yell with excitement. *2:11:02! Holy freakin' cow!* I just beat my record, Southern College's record, and Southern States' record. Pushing myself up out of the lane and water, I'm greeted by my coach and teammates. They embrace me, and we all squeal with excitement.

Once our freak-out moment is over, I look toward the stands to see my entire support system on their feet celebrating. Then, I look to the *#TeamDylan* crowd, and they have their sign hidden and are no longer saying a word. All I can think to myself is mission accomplished as we make our way back to the stands.

My fan club stays where they are this time, even though I know it is about to kill them. They realize if they move, then their fabulous seats will be taken since the meet isn't over, and there are still events to win. We can celebrate later.

Grabbing a towel, I turn to sit down and take my phone from my bag. Of course, there is a text from Cash.

Cash: You were unbelievable! Those ppl shut up quick after turn one! Love u!

Me: :) Love u 2! I'm glad they shut up, & I'm going 2 give them more reason 2 be quiet soon!

We spend the remainder of our time cheering on our teammates and preparing for the relay. We are seated beside Davidson again, and we all look at each other. Nothing like a repeat of last night.

When the individual medley relay is called, we all take our places and blow them out of the water again. This time it is almost too easy. As we glance up to see the clock, I hear that bitch from the locker room making a smart-ass comment. We all turn to look at her.

"Are you still talkin'?" Tori asks firmly.

"I don't know what you're talking about," she says with an eye roll.

That's when Tori looks at me and has that *I'll whoop her ass* look.

"Exactly, you don't know what you're talking about. You know nothing about the situation. Dylan is a piece of work, and if you think your comments bother me, they don't. In fact, I feel sorry for you, because not only are you insecure, you can't put your mouth where the pool is." I walk past her to the stands with my head held high. I take my bag, shower, change, and watch the rest of the meet.

Southern College places first overall in girls. Coach is ecstatic and wants to celebrate, but all I want to do is get back to Southern so I can celebrate with the Kluft girls and Cash Money! Before we leave, I tell my parents bye, and inform Tessa, Dustin, and Cash that I have to ride back with the team.

"Char, I think we're just going to go back to Grassy Pond. Piper can drive your car," Tessa says.

"Why would y'all wanna do that?" I question.

"Probably 'cause I can't get in to Hank's, and even if y'all can sneak me in, there's no way they're going to let Dustin in."

I'm surprised that I hadn't even thought about that. I don't want her to leave, but I have no choice really. "Well, that sucks!"

"Charley!" Mom says. "What am I gonna do with you two?!"

Tessa and I just look at each other and shrug our shoulders.

"I don't want y'all to go, but that does make sense. Piper, will you take the Honda?"

"Yeah."

I give Tessa and Dustin a hug before they leave with my parents.

Cash, Piper, and Joe stop to eat on the way back, and it's going to be a fun night at Hank's Tavern tonight.

We stop to eat on our way back to Southern, and we are able to sit back, relax, and enjoy the time as a team. Coach is the finest lady I know besides my mama. She is classy at all the right times and a little redneck when needed. She knows each of us, and regardless of our pasts, she loves us all. I guess she's like our mama away from home. She is a little cooler than my mama, if I do have to say. 'Cause there's no way my mama wouldn't give me crap if she knew I partied and was hung over. Not to say, she wouldn't fix a killer breakfast to get me over it, but I'd pay one way or the other.

Once we finish eating, Southern picks up the tab, and it's time to get back. I can't wait to be back in Cash Money's arms, let alone spend the night dancing in them. I must be staring out the window when Georgia breaks my thoughts.

"Char, whatcha thinkin' 'bout?"

"Just that I can't wait to go to Hank's tonight."

"Yeah, I bet not!" Tori pipes in.

"Y'all, hush! I mean, I know y'all are jealous of my Cash Money, but he's mine."

After a handful of eye rolls, Georgia asks the question they all wanna know the answer, "So...um...are Piper and Joe an item?" Not really sure how to answer this, I take a second, but that's a second too long because Tori puts in her two cents.

"Oh, they're an item all right! I don't know how exclusive, but they are for sure to-geth-er!"

"Y'all, I don't know the official answer, but I do know they have it bad!" I say.

"Well, let's just see if she does a walk of shame in the morning."

We all chuckle because we know beyond a doubt that is going to happen.

Before we know it, we are pulling into Southern. Coach parks at the gym, and we pile out. She informs us that she will see us for a team meeting next week to discuss off-season workouts and plans for next year, and then she tells us to enjoy the night and to call her if we need a ride.

I text Cash as we make our way back to the dorm. He informs me that they are in Joe's room, and he will come that way. Walking to the dorm, we can hear the party has already begun on campus. Music is being played from dorm to dorm, we can hear people talking, and the stoop is packed with people sitting there with cold ones in their hands already. As we walk up the steps, we are all greeted with congrats, hoots, and hollers. I get the most attention from everyone. We stop and talk for a minute before making our way to Kluft.

Once we are upstairs, we notice Caroline and Hayden waiting on us with Caroline's famous PJ in hand and empty cups. Knowing we can't disappoint them, we each fill a Solo cup and chill

125

for a minute before we head to our rooms and get ready to continue our pre-game before Hank's.

Tossing my bag and coat onto the ground, I honestly want another shower because the smell of chlorine is still very evident on my skin, but I don't know if I have time. Taking a sip of PJ, I toss the thought aside. I begin to look through the closet when there is a light knock on my door. "Come in!" I holler.

Cash, Piper, and Joe enter. They each have a drink, and I know this is going to be an epic night. The question is, who is going to be the DD? Cash typically doesn't drink when I do, but for some reason tonight, we are both letting loose. I can only hope that this is in more ways than one.

"Celebratin,' are we?" I question.

"Well, I figured I could have a couple before we leave then I can drive back," Cash says.

"I have a better idea. Why don't we let Sarah drive the Love Machine, and we all let loose?"

I can see the struggle in Cash's eyes. We both need to let go, but there is the underlying factor that this isn't over with Dylan yet. Piper and Joe look at each other and take a step in the hallway and excuse themselves to Caroline's room.

I set my cup on the dresser and move closer to Cash. Placing my hands on his chest, I look into those eyes that tell me what he's thinking in his soul.

"Cash, one night. We have everyone we need by our sides. He can't touch us tonight. Please, let's forget about everything and live in the moment."

"Char-coal, this is something I promised myself that I'd always do for you. I'll never let anyone hurt you again. *Never*," he says as he brushes his hand in my hair.

Looking into his eyes, I beg him, "Please, Cash Money. Just tonight. Let's forget everything and focus on us because we don't know what's going to happen in the future."

"I *know* what's going to happen in the future, and I'm staring into her eyes right now. I have no doubts about court, our future, or us. You are it. End of story."

I bat my eyelashes and smile a little more seductively, while Cash shakes his head before giving into me, because he knows as well as I do a Southern girl *always* gets her way. Then, he seals his statement with a kiss. Taking me by the hand, we go to see what everyone is doing in Caroline's room.

As we enter, all eyes turn to us. "What?" I question.

Hayden proceeds to say what everyone else is thinking. "So, are y'all finally gonna live a little? Seriously, this mushy lovey-dovey mess is getting old. I mean, it's time to, ya know," she says as she stands and starts to move her hips in a way I never want to see again, but can't help but crack a smile. The entire room erupts in laughter, and I go to fill my cup again. It doesn't take long for the effects of the alcohol to fill my veins. I decide to stop after this cup. I want to have fun, but I still need a little control.

Once we finish our cups, we all excuse ourselves to get ready for Hank's. Cash goes with Joe to his room while Piper and I get ready. This way I can finally talk to her about what is going on. We tell the guys not to be gone long, and as soon as the door is shut, I'm on Piper like white on rice!

"Start talkin'," I say as she begins to grab her clothes from her bag.

"What ever are you talkin' about?" she asks with just a hint of sarcasm.

"You know damn well what I'm talkin' 'bout. Now, spill it."

She plops onto my bed. "Ohmygosh! Char. It. Was. Ah-mah-zing!"

"Uh hum… so, are y'all exclusive?"

"I sure hope so! But anyways, Char, never in my life have I met a guy who can make me feel that way. I mean, I know this is kinda fast, but I totally get what you mean about just knowing when you've found the one."

"It's hard to believe that Little Miss Pull 'Em on a String has found her match!"

"Charley! I can't believe you just called me that, but I guess it's true. I just don't want to leave and go back to school."

"Girl, we're in the same boat except mine is leaving me. It's gonna be fine; at least you have me here. Joe and I might help keep each other sane. I think we need to make this a night to remember, whatcha think?"

"I couldn't agree more," she says as she pulls out a way too short skirt and halter-top.

"You do know it's winter, right?"

"Yup, but I have my man and alcohol to keep me warm." She winks and then begins to get dressed.

I, on the other hand, have to search my closet. *What to wear? What to wear?* As I peruse the closet, nothing catches my eye. Then, I think maybe I should be a little more like Piper. I know it's Hank's, but I'm also with Cash, and I want to make a lasting impression since he's leaving tomorrow.

As I glance over the skirts and tops in my closet, my eyes land on my denim skirt, and I pair it with my camo racer back that I wore my first day on campus. I add my boots to complete the wardrobe. Cash isn't going to know what to do with me.

When I take the outfit from the closet and toss it onto the bed, Piper reads my mind. "I know what you're tryin' to do, but do you think it's gonna work?"

"Hell no, but I have a feeling I might get a tiny piece of action."

"Somethin's better than nothin'," she says.

"Exactly!"

We turn up the iPod and sing a little Pistol Annies when Hayden bursts through the door. "What the hell is this shit?"

"Pistol Annies, ya know Miranda Lambert!" Piper says.

"Um no, but I swear I teleported to like fifty years ago."

"Hayden, you don't know what you're missin'! The Pistol Annies kick ass and take names," I state.

We proceed to sing "Hell on Heels." Hayden just stands there speechless. When the song ends, I wasn't prepared for her revelation.

"Now that's some serious shit! You mean, that's how y'all country girls *really* roll?" she asks in her attempt at a Southern accent.

"Yup, that's how we roll," we say together.

Once we finish getting ready, I send Cash a text, and he informs me that they are on the third floor of Irvin, and it's getting pretty wild around there. *Wild? We might need to check that out.* I tell him we will just come over there. Piper and I gather everyone from Caroline's room and decide one more glass of PJ will set the night off. With the Kluft girls in tow, we make our way to Irvin, and sure enough, when we hit the third floor, wild is an understatement.

Music is blaring through the hall, and the bass is vibrating the windows and echoing down the stairwell. The lights are out, but there are lamps from the dorm rooms to help guide us down the hall. People are everywhere, but as soon as we make our way down the hall, all eyes focus on Piper and me. We all look fabulous for a night at Hank's, but I will admit that Piper and I are a little over the top. That's when I see him. Cash is standing there with a PBR in hand wearing a fitted T-shirt and jeans with his boots and the cutest damn baseball cap ever. Every muscle in his arms is bulging from the shirt, and honestly, I want to bypass Hank's and have an exclusive show in my room. *Wishful thinking... I know.*

As soon as our eyes meet, I grin from ear to ear, and even though I can feel more than his eyes on me, I know that his are the only ones that matter. I walk with confidence, hope, desire, and angst of what the night will hold and what the future will bring us. Cash nudges Joe, but Joe has already noticed Piper as well. Who would have thought the two guys that I tried to have my cake and eat it too are friends, but better yet, we all have found happiness.

Once I'm within arms' length of Cash, his hand extends to mine, and our fingers dance together. I glance into his eyes, and he gives me a wink before whispering into my ear, "You do know you're makin' it hard for me to keep my promise, don't you?"

"Maybe that's what I'm working toward," I say as I whisper into his ear and give it just a little nip. I feel every muscle in Cash's body stiffen. Exactly the reaction I hoped for.

"Char-coal, you better watch it if you know what's good for ya."

"You sure you know what's good for me?"

"I'm just sayin' with you doin' stuff like that, I might get pushed to my limit on what I can say no to."

"Well, then I hope I make you break."

Cash tries to change the subject. Yup, this night is going to be one for the record books because if he's struggling now, I can only imagine what's gonna happen after a night at Hank's.

After finishing our drinks, laughing at some drunk soccer girls, and knowing the time is right, we all stumble our way to the Love Machine. Cash guides me to the van and makes sure I get in gracefully. I probably should have stopped after glass number two, but, oh well. It's too late now.

Our ride to Hank's is loud. Everyone is talking, ya know, the kind when all intoxicated people are trying to out talk each other. At some point, Sarah yells for us all to shut up or we can walk. We try our best to be quiet, but after a minute of silence, it's impossible. Once one chuckle escapes Hayden's lips, we all erupt, and Sarah can't help but laugh as well.

As we pull into Hank's, I notice that nothing has changed. It is still the wooden frame club we all love on a Saturday night. One of the streetlights is flickering, and they have poured new gravel into the parking lot. Sarah pulls us in on two wheels, and we exit and walk toward the entrance.

Cash pulls open the glass door, and this time they make sure to place an "X" on our hands for underage. *Damn.* I look confused when Tori makes it in without an "X." Once we are inside, we make our normal first stop at the restroom, and ask Tori to explain.

"Hey, it pays to have a cousin that could be your twin. I just got in free and can drink."

"You do know you're buying mine, too?" Anna states.

"Already in the works."

Once our makeup is checked, we head to the dance floor. I notice that Cash and Joe are both propped up near the pool table. Piper and I make our way over to them and guide them to the dance floor. It's not like it takes much effort because we all know they both love to dance as much as we do.

As the crowd grows, the closer we all become, and before I know it, there is no space between Cash and me. The DJ continues to play typical Hank's Tavern music where you never know if it's going to be hip-hop or country, but with every beat, my hips match it and Cash follows along. The heat from the crowd coupled with the heat that's building between the two of us is almost enough to make us combust. As the DJ switches up the set, I know the song as soon as I hear the first beat. It's "Bottoms Up" by Brantley Gilbert. This is going to be fun. This song has a slow but evident beat. It's like the perfect country girl's make-a-guy-drool-all-over-ya kinda song, and that is exactly what happens.

Cash sings every word, and I can't help but dance with just a little more emphasis as I roll my hips from left right with my bottom up in exactly the right place. Cash then places his hands on my hips and follows them as they move to the beat of the music. With each word and beat, Cash and I fall more in tune with each other. I lift my hair off my neck as "Damn" escapes his lips. He turns me to face him as he sings directly to me. Every word brings us closer until there is nowhere for me to go. Looking into his eyes, I can see what he wants, and he wants me. I do what any girl in my position would do; I push him to the point that I hope he breaks.

Not being able to fight me any longer, Cash takes the back of my neck and brings me in for a kiss that is filled with want like I've never felt before. I meet him with each move, and before I know it, he is guiding me away from the dance floor and out the back door.

The winter air brushes my glistening skin, but I'm not cold. Instead, I feel a fire burn deep inside. Cash presses me against the outside wall of Hank's. My arms wrap around his neck, and he moves his mouth from my mouth down my neck.

"Hot damn," I say because those are the only words I can manage. My body is starting to have feelings that I never thought could happen, and Cash is struggling to keep his promise as he begins to graze the hem line of my skirt, and as he starts to venture to a place he promised not to go, we are brought back to reality when the back door flies open.

Cash stops what he is doing and leaves his hand on my thigh as his forehead falls against mine. "Damn," he says breathlessly.

"Damn is exactly right," I say quietly.

Cash removes his hand, takes mine in his, and starts to pull me back toward the door. Knowing that's not how I want this to end, I stop him and pull him back toward me, leaving him breathless one more time.

Chapter 20

Sneaking back into Hank's, we find Piper, Joe, and the Kluft girls right where we left them, or at least, where I think we left them. They all have that *what have y'all been up to* look on their faces, but we ignore it and join right in with them dancing and enjoying the remainder of the night with hope that this is just the beginning.

I notice that Georgia is dancing with Tucker again. *Interesting.* I didn't think he had called, but he could turn into Georgia's constant dance partner at Hank's, and who knows, maybe even when we all go out in Charlotte. She looks at me and smiles as she sways her hips back and forth only partially on beat.

I turn my focus back to Cash as we enjoy being Cash Money and Char-coal for the rest of the night. We dance, sing, make out, and can't keep our hands off each other regardless of whether we are dancing with each other or with the Kluft girls.

As last call is announced, I know this night is going to end soon, but I don't want it to. I want it to last forever. Cash must sense my feelings, along with Piper, because she steals me away from Cash for a few moments. We laugh and dance together like we are at the McCracken's farm. She's my best friend. No matter what, Piper is the girl that reads my thoughts, feels my emotions, and knows what to do without saying a word. I can't be happier than I am in this moment with Piper and Cash by my side.

We share the same hometown roots, and that will never change. We have a bond that can't be explained, and I never want it to break.

When Cash has had enough, he steals me back, and just in time. "Let's Get it On" begins to play through the speakers, and a grin escapes Cash in a half-smile as we sway back and forth together, and everyone around us disappears. When the music stops, he and I stand caught in each other's gaze. The house lights come on, and we are all brought back to reality from our hole in the wall escape known as Hank's Tavern. What a night, and it's not over yet.

As we make our way back to campus, Cash never lets go of me. Of course, Hayden wants a Servco hotdog, and all I want to do is be alone with Cash. Sarah does her best to keep Hayden in line and tells her that we are just going back. Of course, Hayden's not having it, and she throws out that she owns the Love Machine, and we will take it wherever she says. Needless to say, we go to Servco, and that early morning snack is fabulous to say the least.

We arrive back on campus around two-thirty. I'm exhausted, and it looks like everyone else is the same way. My body is drained from the meet as well as an epic night out with my friends, but mostly from an emotional roller coaster between Cash Money and me. It has definitely been an eventful night, but in an OMG! I want more kinda way! When Sarah pulls parallel to the stoop, all of us pile out since this is our side of the tracks. Cash guides me out, and Joe does the same with Piper. The Kluft girls go on inside while we stand outside for a few minutes.

Cash stands behind me with his arms wrapped around me. "This is nice," he says.

"Nice?" I question.

"Yeah, the fact that the four of us are standing here without a care in the world, living life like *we* want, and know that we are here for each other regardless of what might come our way."

"Damn right," Joe confirms.

"Awe, y'all are getting so mushy. Stop!" Piper states sarcastically.

"I'm just glad that we have each other. I never thought that Joe and Cash would get along, let alone be friends, and now you and him, Piper," I say with an eyebrow raised. She mouths for me to shut up.

"I don't know about y'all, but I'm exhausted." She tries to change the subject.

"Yeah, and I feel like I smell like Hank's. Yuck! I have to admit; I'm pretty whooped tonight, too," I say.

"You should be. Between the meet and tonight, I don't know how you're still functioning."

"I guess when you have good motivation to stay awake anything's possible." Cash squeezes me just a little bit tighter.

After a few more minutes of pointless conversation and breakfast planning, we go our separate ways.

All I can think of is a nice shower before I crawl into bed with Cash. But, then again, what's the point? He reeks of Hank's, too. As soon as the door is closed to my room, Cash embraces my neck with his rugged hand and brings my lips to his. My body makes a thud sound as he backs me against the door. A giggle escapes my lips, knowing the resident assistant is next door, and that Cash is having as hard of a time as I am with this promise.

He continues to kiss my lips with need and then makes perfect little nibbles all the way behind my ear. Everything in my body tells me this is it, but my mind tells me that he hasn't broken yet. I, on the other hand, am broken into about a million pieces in a good way this time.

"Cashhhh," I say barely audible. "Please."

He shakes his head no, but that doesn't stop him from taking things as far as they can go without us actually breaking his promise. I was almost starting to think he wasn't human, but after tonight, there are no doubts that he's human all right and keeping his promise will be a miracle. After pushing our bodies and mind to the limit, I fall asleep on Cash's bare perfectly carved chest, and I'm in heaven.

As the sunlight begins to creep through my window, I realize this isn't a dream, and I am lying next to the man that has been chosen for me. Even though I hate to admit it, in this moment, I know that we are worth the wait, but will we be able to push the limits without going there?

Chapter 21

Snuggling toward Cash Money as much as possible, I don't want this moment to end. Cash begins to mumble, but I can't make it out. I close my eyes and doze back off for another hour before he wakes me with little minute kisses.

"You better stop that if you know what's good for ya," I mumble.

"What's good for me, huh? I do believe last night you knew what was good for me."

"Cash Money, are you trying to say that was what you wanted? Me to push you to that breaking point, but not go there?"

"I'll never tell," he says as he gives me a peck on the lips and brushes his body across mine as he climbs out of bed.

"Where ya goin'?" I question.

"The little boys' room or more like the little girls' room."

I laugh as Cash excuses himself, and I text Piper. She doesn't respond, so I'm willing to bet they aren't up yet, even though it's getting close to noon.

When Cash returns, he crawls back into bed with me, and we lie there with each other and savor the moment of togetherness.

"Char-coal, I love you. You know that, right?"

"Yeah, why?"

"'Cause there's one thing I need to tell you about…" My senses begin to heighten and an uneasy feeling sweeps over my body.

Pulling myself from his arm, I turn to him. "What do you mean you have something to tell me?"

"Just listen to everything first," he says. I know for a fact that anything that starts with words like that isn't going to be good. In fact, I'm scared that Cash is about to break me. "When you went away to school, I didn't know what to do with myself, knowing everything that had gone on. I had to do everything in my power to know what was really going on with Dylan. I didn't tell you, but Dustin and I started hanging out." *Well, that's no shocker.* "But, what we didn't tell you is that we also started hanging out with Trent. I had to *know* how they did things. With Dustin on my side, Trent trusted us and we know what they use, how they get it, and how they get the girls to trust them."

Horror flashes across my face. Please God don't tell me what I think he's about to say. "Don't go there, Charley. I'm not a monster, and you know it." Taking a deep breath, I sit up and continue to listen to a story that I don't want to believe. "One night, the night I went out with Tessa and Sally came, we had them play along. Dustin and I gave Trent the whole package, made him think we were going to give them "Z," and more importantly, Sally and Tessa went along with it."

"What do you mean they went along with it'?"

"Charley, we did everything Trent told us to do, but with one minor change. When we put the "Z" into their drink, we actually switched the drinks. We drank it."

"You did *what*?!" I shout.

"I couldn't do that to those two, and if we were going to do that, we had to have two people we trusted with us."

"Question." Cash waits for it. "How did you make it home driving if y'all drank it? It took no time for that to have an effect on me."

"Well, Dustin and I split the dose between us first of all, and we were in my truck. As soon as we were out of sight of the party, Tessa took the wheel. Then, they took us to the club to sleep it off."

"I just don't understand why?"

"Char-coal, at that point, you weren't taking action, and if you weren't, then I had to do something."

"So, why are you just now telling me?"

"Because I have a feeling that Dylan is going to try to use that against me in court. I'm ahead of

144

him, though. My lawyer already knows, and Dustin and I have video of deals made in Trent's house, along with documentation of what we were doing. We have pictures of us that night. We have everything that the court will need to stop this entire operation."

Letting my tense body relax, I realize that Cash didn't break me; he freed me once again. He truly is my knight in an F250 and a pair of Carhartts. A smile spans across my face.

"You do realize that I thought you were about to break me into a million pieces?"

No longer wanting to have any distance between us, Cash moves to sit directly in front of me, brushing my hair behind my ear. "I could never break you because that would demolish my soul. Our souls are intertwined forever, and what you feel, I feel."

Looking into his eyes, I see deep into his soul, and I know he speaks the truth. Regardless of everything going on in my life, he has never lied to me. Placing my hand on his cheek, I bite my lip and agree silently as we remove all space between us. His lips are light yet needy. We move in perfect unison, as we know that there are no walls between us, and we make use of every moment we have until my phone begins to play "Hell on Heels," and Piper interrupts us.

"Hey," I say shortly.

"Did I just interrupt something?"

"What do you think?" I ask in a smart-ass tone.

"Maybe Cash needs to give in so you won't be such a smart ass." She laughs.

"Haha! You know better than that. So, what are y'all doin'?" I question.

"Finally moving. I guess it's safe to say we missed breakfast, huh?"

"Yeah, but it's okay. I needed to sleep in. We can always go to IHOP or something if y'all still want breakfast."

I hear Piper ask Joe what he wants, and I glance at Cash who basically doesn't care what we do as long as we are together.

"That sounds great. Give us about thirty minutes, and we'll be ready to go." We hang up, and I fall right back into Cash Money's arms. "We have thirty minutes." I wink.

"Well, how about you just let me hold you for a few minutes before we get ready?"

"Sounds absolutely perfect."

Cash holds me in his arms, and we talk about random stuff. When we get up, I take a super quick shower, get ready, and throw my hair up into a messy bun. Cash is packed and ready to go, and just seeing him standing there with his bags makes my heart sink.

"Hey, no need for that, Char-coal. These next few weeks will be over before you know it. Then, hopefully, court will be behind us, and we will be spending a weekend away at the Florida Georgia Line concert. That brings a smile to my face. I hope Cash gets off easy, and I don't have to take Tessa instead. "Whatcha thinkin'?" he asks.

"That I sure hope Tessa doesn't have to go with me to the concert."

Dropping his bag to the floor, he walks toward me, pulls me in for a strong hug, and tells me that he promises it will be us. There is one thing I know about Cash; he always keeps his promises.

"Now, let's go. I feel a big ol' stack of pancakes callin' my name," he says as he takes me by the hand, and we make our way to meet Piper and Joe.

They are waiting for us by Joe's Jeep. Knowing that Piper has to leave, she drives separately from Joe. I decide to ride with Cash since I know I can ride back to campus with Joe.

After sliding into the middle of the front bench seat, I rest my head on Cash's shoulder for part of the ride. Cash turns up the radio to our favorite country station. We sing every word that comes through the speakers, but when Brantley Gilbert begins to play, I think my face turns a million shades of red.

"Whatcha blushin' for?"

"I have no idea what you're talkin' about, Cash Money."

"I know exactly why you're blushin', but there's no reason for it. Honestly, that's one of the highlights of our relationship."

I gasp. "And to think I was really starting to wonder if I could make you give in just a teeny tiny bit."

"I'd have given in a long time ago, but there's always a time and a place for everything."

"Why do you have to always be right? It drives me crazy."

"Hopefully, it just makes you crazier for me," he says with a smile.

"Oh, it does." I give him a few kisses on his neck as he is driving, and he informs me I better stop before we wreck.

As we pull into IHOP, we are greeted by Piper and Joe having a little "them time" in Joe's Jeep. I'm not really sure how they got here before us, but, oh well.

"Um, do we interrupt them, or just go on in?" Cash questions as he points to them.

"I'll text her." After a brief moment, they break apart and exit the Jeep.

We enter with a little awkward silence as we are seated. After the waitress takes our drink and food order, things get back to normal. We just cut up and enjoy the next hour before we all have to go our separate ways.

After we eat, we hang out outside as we avoid saying goodbye. When the inevitable is upon us, each couple goes their separate ways after I tell Piper bye. Joe and Piper go to her car, and Cash and I go to his truck.

As he places his arms around my waist, he asks, "You remember the last time I told you bye in a parking lot?"

As I slide my arms around his neck, I reply, "I sure do. That was the moment I realized we would never be over."

"What do you mean that's the moment you knew?"

"Cash Money, I could fight us from now until the cows come home, but what's the point? That day when I drove off and back to school, deep down I knew that even if I wanted to be on my own, you would be at the finish line. I love you, and I always have regardless of how stubborn I am. It was just something I had to do. You. Are. My. Forever."

He tilts his head to meet mine, and we don't talk with words, but with actions until I hear Joe clearing his throat.

"Sorry to break up the party, but Piper's about to head out. Looking up, I see her backing out of the space. She has her window down and is yelling bye to us as she pulls onto the main road. *Gosh, I love that girl.* Cash places his arm around my shoulder and pulls me in close as we wave goodbye to her.

"She sure is somethin'," I say.

"Y'all have no idea." Joe smirks.

"Just give me a minute, and I'll be ready. Okay, Joe?"

"Just meet me at the Jeep. Cash, I'll take care of her, and I'll see ya soon," he says as they shake hands.

As Joe turns to go to his Jeep, I realize that this is it. The next time I see Cash will either be in court or the night before the hearing.

"Don't. Char-coal. Don't," Cash says in a hushed tone.

Trying my best to force back tears, I shake my head okay, but inside, I never want to leave him. I want to throw away everything I've worked toward and spend every moment possible with him until the future is decided.

"Just think. The next time you see me, this will be at an end. Dylan will have his verdict and so will I. We will come out on top, so don't you worry your cute little ass about it. Do you understand me?"

"Okay." I quiver.

"Promise me," he says confidently.

"I promise."

"I love you, Charley Anne Rice, and when this is over, our life is truly going to start." Then, he kisses me deep into my soul.

"I love you too, Cash Porter Montgomery, and I can't wait to spend every mornin' wakin' up beside you, and when I close my eyes at night, you're there, too." He hugs me tight and kisses me once more before he walks me to Joe's Jeep.

Cash opens the door like the true Southern gentleman he is and guides me to the seat before he closes the door. I roll down the window, and he leans in and brushes his lips against mine one last time then he tells us bye, turns, and walks to his truck. I swear nothing can brighten my day better than watching him walk away, even though it breaks my heart because an ass shouldn't look that good in a pair of Carhartts.

Joe starts to laugh. "What?" I ask.

"You got it bad."

"Whatever, like you can talk," I banter right back.

"You got a point."

He puts the Jeep in reverse, and we make our way back to Southern. The entire way back, I play twenty questions with him about Piper. By the time we finish, I've embarrassed him so much that he doesn't answer the questions, but I keep them coming anyway. Finally, I stop because he's starting to get pissed off. Personally, I think it's funny. Him, not so much.

"On a serious note, Jackalope Joe, if you hurt her, I'll kill ya. Ya got it?"

"If it was any other girl, I might not take you seriously, but I saw the line of trophies hanging in the living room at your parents' house. I don't doubt you one bit, but I promise not to hurt her. If anything, I'm worried about her hurting me."

That kinda stung when Joe said it because I know Piper. She's head over heels for him, but she also has never been one to settle down. She's usually on to the next guy when she gets bored, but she also has never stood up for a guy like she did for Joe over the break with me. I know that there is more than just moving on.

"I know her, and I can promise you this. She has *never* been this way over *any* guy. I believe you're safe. Hell, if she hurts you, I just might whoop her ass." I laugh.

152

"Uh, Squirrel, let's don't. That would revoke my man card," he says like he's wounded.

"True."

Before we know it, we are crossing the railroad tracks onto campus. Joe parks, and I tell him bye. As I start to walk to my dorm, he hollers at me. I turn around, and he's walking toward me. *Confused. That's me.*

"I wasn't sure when I should give this to you, but I figured I better go ahead," he says as he pulls a folded piece of paper from his pocket. Slowly, he hands it to me.

"What is it?" I question.

"It's from Cash. He wanted you to read it after he left."

"Left? What do you mean 'left'?" Panic sets in my tone.

"Charley, don't go there. I meant when he went back home."

"Oh, okay." I grip it tighter in my hand. "Thanks," I say as I turn to leave, but decide to ask one more question. "Hey Joe, do you really think he's going to be all right?"

"I don't think he's the one I'm going to have to worry about. Squirrel, just promise me no matter the outcome that you don't do anything stupid. No more plans. You got me?"

Trying to avoid tears, I agree quickly and turn to go to my room. My hands begin to tremble just thinking about what might be in that note. I want to open it, but I'm scared. *Why am I scared to open something from my Cash Money?* Trying to be incognito from the Kluft girls, I sneak into my room to see what's going on, but realize that Georgia has already spotted me.

"Char, are you okay? I mean, besides the fact that Cash has gone home."

Shaking my head no, my face scrunches together as I force back tears. She sees the note in my hand.

"What's that?" Georgia questions.

"I don't know," I say within a sob.

She approaches me and takes the note. "Do you want me to read it?"

"No, I'm just scared."

Georgia guides me into my room and closes the door. "Char, I don't know much about love, but I do know this. He. Loves. You. That's all you need to think about. Whatever is in this letter is going to confirm that."

Using my sleeve to wipe away the tears, I answer her, "I hope so."

"I know so," she says with a mischievous grin. This makes me smile because whatever is going on here she knows as well, even if she tried to act clueless a minute ago.

"I'll leave you alone a minute," she says as she hands the note back to me and then goes to her room.

After grabbing a tissue, I unfold the paper and begin to read the words from my soul mate.

To my Char-coal,

I know by now you are probably a crying and slobbering mess, and I'm sorry to have made you cry, but those are all the tears you will ever shed over me. This letter is about firsts. I didn't know how to tell you what I really feel about everything going on, so I thought I'd try this.

For starters, you are everything that matters to me. Without you in my life, I serve no purpose. You give me a reason to wake up each morning. Knowing that you are my future is what gets me through the day and through all this mess that's going on now.

I promised you that I would come out on top, and I know that I will. When the judge sees the evidence, my record, and that what I did was to protect you, I know they will be on our side. I know

155

I won't get off completely, but the moment that I can walk out as a free man is the day that I will never leave your side.

Until that day, I want you to live life to the fullest, enjoy the Kluft girls, keep Joe straight, kick ass in the pool, and let your light shine to everyone you meet. You are a one-in-a-million girl, and I can't believe that you are mine from now until eternity. I love you, Charley Anne Rice, and when this is over, I'm never letting you go.

Now, quit sulking, smile that heart-warming smile, and have fun because that's what college is about. I'll see you in two weeks.

Love always and forever and ever,

Your Cash Money

Smiling that heart-warming smile is exactly what I do. Glancing in the mirror, I look like a semi hit me, but I don't care. I open the door only to be greeted by the Kluft girls with open arms.

"'Bout damn time. We got shit to do and take names," Tori says smartly.

"Whatcha mean?"

"We are about to have one hell of a time for the next two weeks because I have a feeling when this is over, Cash isn't going to let you outta his sight."

"Sounds like fun to me!" I say excitedly.

"So, have you heard of Gravity Hill?" Tori questions.

"Um, no. Please tell me it's not some ride at the local county fair?"

With an eye roll, Tori fills me in. "Gravity Hill is this hill in the middle of freakin' nowhere. People say that if you put baby powder on your bumper and turn off your car when you get to the bottom, there will be fingerprints left in the powder."

"What? Is that not just from what falls off the back of the car?"

"Hell, I don't know, but it sounds like something fun to me. So, are you in?"

"Why not. Who has baby powder?" I ask.

We all look at each other and then Caroline speaks up. "I do."

"Why in this world would you have baby powder in your dorm room?" Anna smarts at her.

"Y'all, this Southern Belle's feet cannot sweat! I glisten, remember!" Caroline says in a sweet Southern drawl.

"Only Caroline."

Trying to get us back on track, I ask, "Do we have to do this at dark, midnight, or before sunrise?"

"Midnight," Tori states confidently. "Tonight, girls. It's on. We are living it up for the next two weeks. Everyone game?"

"Hell to tha yeah!" Hayden yells, and we mimic her.

After that decision is made, I check to see if Cash has made it home yet. Instead of texting him, I call.

He answers before the first ring is complete in song. "Go ahead and call me, call me, call me. You don't have to worry 'bout it baby," he sings the words to his ringtone.

"No, I don't have to worry about it because I've got my heart-warming smile and a man that loves me for eternity."

"You read the letter, huh?"

"I did."

"You freaked out, though, didn't you?" I pause, and that is all Cash needs to know that he was right. "I know you too well. You know that, right?"

"I probably wouldn't have if Joe would have given it to me straight, but it was almost like he was unsure of when to give it to me."

"That's probably because I told him to feel when he thought the moment was right."

"Oh, well, just so you know. Georgia had it written all over her face that she knew something, but that has to be the sweetest thing I have ever read in my life. I promise to live life to the fullest for these two weeks, and then it's you and me against whatever is thrown at us."

"Damn right."

"Are you home yet?"

"Just about. I'm hittin' the Grassy Pond stoplights now."

"Hey, Cash Money."

"Yeah."

"I love you. I know those are three little words, but there aren't any words that can come close to how I feel about you.

"I understand completely. I pray every night and thank God that He brought you into my life when we were kids."

"You're makin' us sound so old." I giggle.

"You know what I mean, Char-coal."

"I do, and this serious thing you have going for you is way past sexy."

"Well, you keep those thoughts to yourself until we're together, and then you can tell me in person."

"I like that plan, but that sure is gonna be hard."

We make small talk as Cash drives to his farm, and I fill him in on tonight's event. He doesn't believe me, and frankly, I think it's a crock of shit as well. Regardless, I'm up for something adventurous.

As Cash pulls into his driveway, we say our goodbyes, yet again. He makes me promise to let him know about Gravity Hill later tonight. Hanging up the phone is hard, but I know that each time we disconnect, I'm one time closer to forever.

Chapter 22

As midnight approaches, we are all decked out like we are going on a robbery, not going to check out a crazy legend that has been told from generation to generation. We pile into Tori's Explorer. For some reason, the Love Machine is out of commission tonight, or maybe it's because this is Tori's crazy idea.

"So, do we have a clue what we are supposed to do?" Anna asks.

"From what I understand, we put the car at the top of the hill, and then one of us puts the baby powder on the bumper, and we just roll," Tori states.

"Aight, so I'm not trying to be the party pooper, but there has to be more to it than that," I say.

Tori continues, "Someone said something about you roll up, and if the spirits feel the need to move you, they will. That's all people have said."

Uncertain of how to respond, I leave it at that as we make our way up the two-lane highway, making a few turns and crossing the county lines.

Tori begins to get excited when she sees random spray paint on signs, and we all figure it out when we notice the lines sprayed on the road of where to start. To me, this feels like snipe hunting. If you know what that is, you know we're about to get made to look like fools.

As we reach the top of the hill, Tori does a three-point turn and puts the car in park. She then looks around to see who wants to get out and put the baby powder on the bumper.

"Fine, I'll do it," I say, because to be honest, I want to see what it looks like before this crazy train is over.

"I wanna see, too," Georgia says and follows me, and then everyone is out of the car. Once the powder is in place, we pile back inside. We say a little prayer, and Tori puts it in neutral. The car picks up speed, but not once does she touch the brake or steering wheel. *How in the world have we not run off the road yet?* The car reduces speed as we go back up the next hill, and it begins to slide back to the valley between the two hills, stopping dead center.

Looking around at each other, we know that we are the laughing stock of Southern, but then it happens. The car begins to climb the hill. My eyes dart to Georgia, Caroline, Anna, and up front to Tori. She is as white as a sheet, and we all are speechless.

Once we reach the peak, the car stops, and Tori throws it in park and jumps out. I don't know if I want to get out of the safety of this car, but I'm supposed to live on the edge for two weeks, so here it goes. Throwing the door open, I hurry to the back to see what Tori sees. *Holy shit!* Sure enough, there are two sets of handprints in the baby powder. All the powder is still in place.

"Never in a million years, Tori."

"I'm having the same thought. You got your phone, Char? Take a pic."

"I do, and thanks to the flash, we have evidence for when everyone calls bullshit."

As we make our way back to the car, everyone is dying to know what happened. When I show them the picture, they have to see for themselves, and we talk a mile a minute the entire drive back.

Once we get back to campus, the stoop has several stragglers drinking a few cold ones on a Sunday night. We stop and chat for a couple of minutes before returning to our rooms. I text Cash the picture, and of course, he calls me for the details. He also doesn't hang up until he hears me asleep on my end.

From Monday through Thursday, we aren't too adventurous due to class, but that's not to say we don't drink vodka in our Kool-Aid before class on an unusually warm afternoon. It makes for interesting note taking. At night, we make up our own fun whether it's sliding in our socks down the hall or karaoke from the stoop, and when Georgia does get that call from Tucker, we are the most annoying friends possible. Needless to say, she still scored herself a date, and that is going to be a date she's not going to forget if the Kluft girls have anything to do with it.

"Hey, Georgia. Where's he takin' you?" I ask her as she finishes the touches on her makeup with a lip pop.

"I think we're going to see some new action movie or something and out to eat. Why? What are y'all gonna do?"

"I think we're just going to hang out at the stoop tonight."

Georgia places her hands on her hips. "Char, you do know that's not being adventurous, right?"

"You know as well as I do that you never know what's going to happen there," I reply with the same body language.

"True."

About that time, there's a light knock on her door, and we see Tucker standing there. He isn't tall, but definitely not short by any means. He's got a body to die for. I figured that out before break at Hank's, and if he's taking out Georgia, that means he must really like her. The question is, will he still like her when they get back tonight?

As they leave, we give them all kinds of hell. The funny thing is, as Georgia gets embarrassed, Tucker dishes it right back out at us. I think I like him already.

After Georgia is out of sight, Hayden clasps her hands together and rubs them quickly. I can see the wheels turning. "So, y'all up for a good prank?" she questions.

"She's gonna kill us, ya know," I say. "But, I'm totally in. Whatcha got in mind?"

"I'm thinking fifty-two card pickup, but in dorm room way," Hayden says.

As confusion covers our faces, Hayden gives us a big huff before she explains what we are going to do when we break into Georgia's room, which isn't hard since she leaves it unlocked all the time. We proceed to turn everything she owns backwards. I do mean everything— dresser, refrigerator, microwave, lamp, and then we take it to the next level.

"Hummm, what can we use?" Caroline thinks out loud.

"Y'all! Check out these lights!" I say as I hold up two circle lights that you press on and off.

"I've got an idea. Let's lay this futon out," Anna says. She goes to Georgia's underwear drawer and pulls out the skimpiest pair of panties and matching bra. She takes them to the bed, sets them in the middle, along with placing the lights within the bra cups, and turns them on. We all burst out laughing. "Hey Tori, you got your stash?"

"Yeah." She makes a quick trip to her room and returns with a handful of condoms.

"Oh, my! She's gonna be pissed!" I laugh.

"I know, right? But, I can't wait to see her face," Anna says. "Where's that disco lamp?"

"It's in my room from the last pre-game." When Caroline returns with it, she's also carrying a pair of shiny, new handcuffs. After placing everything perfectly on the futon, we cut off the lights and go to Caroline's room to enjoy a Friday night and wait for the main event to return a little later.

We spend the next two hours playing *Never Have I Ever*. I only drink one glass of PJ and then turn to Choice Cherry Gold after that. Knowing that it has got to be close to time for Georgia to return, we check out who is on the stoop. I see Joe. *Bingo!*

"Hey, y'all. Excuse me. I think I have our lookout." I make my way out to Joe, and as I approach him, he stops mid-conversation.

"Squirrel, you got that look. What's goin' on? Everything okay?" he questions like a big brother.

"It's perfect, but I do need your help with just a little something." Pulling him to the side, I tell him what we've been up to, and he has the same reaction that I did. She's gonna kill us, but of course, he'll play along, too. He agrees to text me

166

when they are walking toward the stoop to give us time to turn on the "boob" lights, and then I go back upstairs.

Within ten minutes, I get a text from Joe.

Joe: Let those lights shine!

Me: Gotcha!

Tori hurries across the hall and hustles back to Caroline's room. What I hadn't prepared for was the loud bass of music bumping from her room. "What? We needed the full effect. Caroline, turn ours up too, so Georgia doesn't notice at first." Caroline turns up the dial, and Katy Perry's "Dark Horse" is all I can hear.

Georgia and Tucker wave as they walk by, and we try our best not to blow our cover. As soon as she's past us, we jump up and hustle to the doorway to see what happens next. She turns the doorknob and instantly flushes beet red. A look of confusion is written all over her face. Tucker doesn't say anything, but you can tell it's caught him off guard as well.

Georgia turns off the radio and then flips on the lights. As she starts to turn around to confront us, we beat her to it.

"We just thought we'd help with the postdate show. Y'all like it?" Tori states more than questions.

Georgia tries to speak, but it's a blubbering mess. Tucker, on the other hand, nails it. "It would have been perfect if it was a pair of thongs."

Her mouth falls open, and she manages to ask one question, "How did you know when we'd be back?" As I start to explain, I'm cut off.

"'Cause I was the lookout," Joe says as he peeks from around the stairwell. He turns to us. "Y'all didn't think after they made it in the door I was just gonna hear about this secondhand, did ya?"

"Of course not," I say.

"I appreciate y'all trying to help me out, but next time, just let me handle it," Georgia says proudly.

We leave them alone and go back to Caroline's room, and Joe joins us, too. We spend the next thirty minutes reliving what just happened. Then, we enjoy the night until we can't keep our eyes open. We excuse ourselves one by one and go to our rooms or someone else's. I most definitely go back to my room and dream of my Cash Money.

The next morning, I wake up to a phone call from Piper who is hysterical. I'm afraid to ask what has happened, because I can probably guess. She got drunk and kissed a guy. That's like her freakin' trademark.

"Piper, calm down. What's wrong?"

"Char, last night when I was out, this guy kept trying to buy me drinks. I let him buy me one, and of course, I got it from the bartender, but he wouldn't leave me alone. After a while, he finally got my drift, or at least I thought, and then I figured it out. Something about him seemed off. What if he was the guy that took my picture that Dylan sent you? He has always tried to talk to me, and I have always blown him off. What if he tries to hurt me?"

Not knowing exactly what to say, I take a deep breath. "Piper, did he try anything?"

"No, after the one drink and me being a total bitch, he left me alone. Last night, I didn't think much about it, but this morning that thought woke me up."

"Have you talked to Joe?" I ask.

"Hell no! He'd be down here and ready to beat someone's ass. I need someone that can help me talk though it."

"Aight, so here's what I think. Yes, it can be a possibility, but it's unlikely. I wouldn't want to toss it to the side, but I also wouldn't freak myself out about it. If he took your hint, then let it go. Keep your guard up and tell someone there you trust. That way if you go out, and he's there, there's another set of eyes on him. And, I would tell Joe. Don't keep it from him. He's got a good head on his shoulders. Just tell him to listen to everything first."

"That was kinda my thought, too. I just needed to hear it from someone else. I've been on edge so much since I got back. I mean, knowing what I thought was everything and then knowing what I didn't know existed has been harder than I thought."

"I'm sorry I haven't been a better friend. This affects you too, and sometimes I just think about myself in the situation."

"Don't even say that, Char. Your situation is important. This is minor compared to what you've experienced. Thanks for listenin' this mornin'. Love ya."

"Love ya, too. Now, call Joe," I demand.

I hang up and roll back over, but I'm unable to sleep with the thought that Piper might be right.

Chapter 23

Throwing my covers off me, I get out of bed, unable to shake that thought from my mind. No one, and I mean *no one*, better mess with Piper. I grab my shower caddy, dollar flip-flops, and towel, praying a shower will clear my mind and I won't do anything drastic.

As I stand in my room toweling off my wet hair, I hear a knock and then Joe's voice. When I open the door, it's very evident that he has spoken to Piper and is a total wreck. He comes in and takes a seat on my bed.

"Joe, don't think the worst," I state as calmly as possible.

"What do you mean? You know damn well as I do that something's not right."

Everything within my soul tells me that something is wrong, but I don't want to freak him out anymore. It's no use because he can see in my delayed reaction that something is wrong.

"I knew it. You think it, too," he says as he slams his hand on my mattress.

"Listen, I think something is off, but I don't want to jump to conclusions. I also don't want Piper scared to go out of her dorm room or live life. We need to see what we can find out."

"Now, how the hell are we gonna do that? We are here, and she is there," he says as he speaks with his arms.

I pace the floor for a moment, and then it dawns on me. "You said you met Dylan during Senior Week. Was there anyone you remember that was going to school with Piper? That might be where we need to start."

Joe takes out his phone and begins to scroll through his Facebook friends, and when I think we are at a loss, he looks up. He passes me the phone, and I look at it. The guy in the picture has skin that has been kissed by the sun and shaggy, yet sexy, dirty blonde hair, and hazel eyes. He is very much eye candy. I read his name. Blanton Marks. *Doesn't ring a bell to me.* I pass the phone back to Joe.

"Blanton Marks goes to the community college there. He was with Trent at the beach. I thought it was weird to have them together, but they said they grew up together."

"I totally forgot that Trent moved to Grassy Pond from down east when he was in middle school, so that is a possibility. Should we send his pic to Piper?"

"I think so, but let's call and explain first."

After explaining our hypothesis to Piper, Joe texts it to her while she remains on the line with me. She pauses to look at it, and a gasp is all we hear.

172

"That's him, y'all. Ohmygawd, that's him. What am I gonna do?"

Joe snatches the phone from me, and I know that he's going to take control of this situation just like he did Study Day when I thought my world was crashing down.

"Baby, listen to me. Don't freak out. I have an idea." He waits for her to quit hyperventilating before speaking again, "You usually see him out on the weekends, right?"

"Yeah, usually Saturday night at the Handlebar. He's a local, and they are all the time inviting us to parties and stuff at the beach. We never go 'cause something is just off about it all."

"How about I'm taking you out Saturday night? You show me a good time at *your* college. I get done with class at noon Friday. Conditioning is that morning, so I can leave as soon as class is over. Will that work?"

"I'd love for you to come see me, but I also don't want any trouble."

"Oh, there's going to be no trouble because when I see him out, I'm going to let him know you are *my* girl and that I know his game. That should stop it, because from what I remember that week, he's a follower, not a leader. If he knows Dylan's in trouble, he's gonna stop."

Joe turns to me. "Do you want to go?"

173

"I'd love to, but I'm not sure. Since I have to go back home next week for court, I might need to stay here, but… I don't want you to have to go by yourself. Let me think it over."

Joe finishes talking to Piper and hands me the phone again. She tells me to stay at Southern. She knows that I'm torn, and knowing her, she honestly wants alone time with Joe, and who can blame her?

After I hang up with Piper, Joe and I really talk about what he thinks will happen. He was honest with Piper, but he did say things might get a little messy if Blanton doesn't listen. Then, he realizes it would be better if I stayed away. I don't need to be involved with anything Dylan related until this hearing is over.

Joe returns to his dorm, and I call Cash and fill him in. He's not happy to say the least. In fact, he thinks we both should go with Joe. I demand that we don't because we can't risk what conflict it could cause for next Thursday. He agrees unwillingly.

Spending the remainder of my Sunday keeping myself busy, I rearrange my room, clean, grocery shop, and map out my week. It's going to be a nerve-racking week for not only me but also everyone I know. The next eleven days are going to build more and more anxiety of going home and walking into that courthouse to face Dylan Sloan.

Surprisingly, the week flies by, and I meet Joe after class on Friday before he leaves to go see Piper. My body feels like it has been wadded up, tossed around, and put back together as he leaves. I'm terrified of the possible outcomes for him tomorrow. He has so much going for him; I just hope his past doesn't come back to haunt him.

"Hey, can you give this to her?" I ask Joe as I pass him a small bag.

He looks at me with a smirk. "Fun Dip? Choice Cherry Gold?"

"Yup, it's kinda our thing. They make everything better. If I can't be there, these are the next best things," I say with a shoulder shrug.

"Oh, *really*? I thought I was the next best thing!"

"You're probably right, but this is my way of being there. Now, take care of her."

Joe gives me a hug, and I push back the tears as he gets into his Jeep. As Joe pulls away, I go and sit at the picnic table to clear my head. I pull out my phone and text Cash. I need to see him. It's not a want. I need him to hold me.

Me: Whatcha doin' Cash $?

After what feels like forever, he replies.

Cash: Sorry, I was putting a new belt on the tractor. What's up?

Me: I need you.

My phone rings. As I connect, he is already speaking.

"What do you mean you *need* me?" he asks with worry in his voice.

"Cash Money, I need *you.*"

"Oh my lord, Char-coal. I was about to haul ass to the truck! You can't text things like that."

"What? Just 'cause I'm not in trouble you're not gonna come to my rescue?"

"Oh, I'll come to your rescue, but you better really *need* me."

"You know what I *need*? I need your strong, hard working, and perfectly sculpted arms wrapped around me when I close my eyes tonight. Do you think that's possible?"

A low growl escapes his voice like he is fighting an inner battle. "Char-coal, I can't. I have to stay home and help my parents this weekend. I know it's the last weekend before everything, but I owe it to them, especially since I don't know what will happen after Thursday. Dad has me going to a sale this weekend with him, and then making sure everything is in line to get ready to plant over the next couple of weeks. I'm so sorry."

My heart sinks a little, but I also know that he's speaking the truth. He has a major role on the farm, and if he does have to do time, he can't leave his dad high and dry.

"I understand. I don't like it, but I understand," I say with sadness in my voice.

"Believe me. If I had a choice between selling cattle or lying next to you tonight... the cows win hands down." He tries to say it seriously.

"Cash Porter Montgomery, no, you just didn't!"

He bursts out laughing. "You're right. I'd choose you hands down no matter the other choice."

"Even if it was Carrie Underwood?"

"Damn straight, I'd choose you over her. Because for me, she's not perfect, and you *are* perfect for me."

My heart melts once again for Cash Money. We talk for a few minutes before I let him get back to work, and I promise to have a good time this weekend.

As I walk upstairs, Caroline and Georgia are standing in the hallway. They are propped against the wall with their arms crossed like they are ready to pounce on somebody.

"Um, are y'all okay?" I ask.

"Hell no, we aren't! What's going on with Joe?" Caroline quizzes.

"What do you mean? He's going to see Piper," I say nonchalantly.

Georgia pushes herself off the wall, thinks, and then speaks, "You better tell me *why* he's going. Something's up… I can feel it."

"Come on. I need some Fun Dip and a Choice Cherry Gold," I say as I walk back into my room.

"Oh, shit. This ain't good!" Georgia states as they follow me into the room, grabbing their own Fun Dip and drink.

"Spill it!" Caroline announces.

"Okay, I didn't want y'all to worry, but someone's messin' with Piper. Joe and I have put the pieces together, and he pretty much is going to let the guy know it this weekend. Nothing major, but I didn't want to go because it can cause issues next week."

"Nothin' major, my ass! I can't believe you think Georgia and I would buy this bullshit," Caroline says loudly.

At this point, I know I can't hide anything from these two. Out of everyone, they are the most like me. "Fine. It's a guy named Blanton Marks. I don't know him, but he grew up with Trent. He's been makin' moves on Piper and her friends for a while, but this past weekend, he totally freaked her out. We've been trying to keep her from worrying, but Joe and I knew something wasn't right. Between my knowledge of Grassy Pond and Joe being there Senior Week, we were able to figure it out. I guess you'd say he and Joe are acquaintances. He's hoping to tell him the game's over. I'm just praying that he doesn't get himself in trouble. He can't afford for that to happen."

"What do you mean he can't afford to get in trouble?" Caroline questions.

"That's a story for another day. Just know that Joe's had it rough growing up. He's the perfect image of what a pretty boy would be like, but life's not always been nice to him. He's lucky Southern gave him a shot. Not to mention, he has one kick-ass grandma who believed in him when everyone else tossed him to the side."

Georgia and Caroline's eyes float back between each other's. "Y'all, it's okay. This weekend is going to be epic, and after next week, I'll have my life back!"

"Char, you do know that it could get continued, or they might actually have to take it to trial, right?" Georgia says, stating what I've been thinking.

I don't want to think about that. I just want to have my life back, and I want Thursday to be that day. I have to testify in court, lay all my business out for everyone to hear, and after that point, if I have to do it again, I will, but I will be free regardless of whether the decision has been made.

"I know, Caroline, but once I say this out loud, for me, I *will* be free. When I told the police, it was hard, but after I did, it felt like an elephant was lifted off me."

"I gotcha. So, what are we going to do to make this weekend one we don't forget?"

We sit there a minute racking our brains before Caroline jumps up and gets beyond excited. "I've got an idea! Y'all know how much fun Hank's is on Saturday, right? What if we create our own club here tonight?"

"You do realize we could all get kicked out for something like that, don't you?" I state.

"Y'all know as well as I do that Mr. Wannabe Cop isn't going to do anything. Now, our RA could be another story, but y'all know she's got some nerd in her life now and hasn't been around as much," Caroline informs us.

"She's got a point, Charley. We can totally get away with it, and you know the guys' RA downstairs couldn't care less."

Knowing that this will be a night to remember, I agree. "Sounds like a plan to me. Let's tell the rest of the Kluft girls. We have less than eight hours to turn this place into a club."

We go to Tori's room and tell them our idea. They are game, so we make our to-do list while Tori calls their beer guy. We decide how we are going to decorate and then rummage through our rooms to see what we can find. Each of us brings the items into the hall. When we look around, we don't have much of anything except a disco ball, three sets of sheer purple curtains, a cooler, leftover Christmas party decorations, and that's about it.

"You guys, I think we're going to have to do better than this! We need to go to shopping or at least to the dollar store," Anna states the obvious.

"We can roll with this," Tori says. "I'm thinkin' use what we have and then make a trip."

We plan out where we will hang the curtains, old decorations, and whatever else we can find. Then, we cut off the lights and turn on the disco ball. *Pretty impressive to say the least.*

Georgia starts to laugh. "It looks like someone threw up purple in here!"

"Yeah, it looks like either My Little Pony or a Care Bear took over." Tori cackles.

"Yeah, Club Purple! The place to dance like no one's watching and leave everything to the imagination!" Anna says a little too seductively.

"Ohmygosh, y'all, that is freakin' hilarious!" I say with a laugh.

With time to spare, we turn off the disco light and order pizza while we get ready. We all send texts to everybody we know. Tonight is going to be a blast. I have a group of great friends that make their own fun, and I wouldn't change my world right now if my life depended on it!

With the sun starting to set, I call Cash. By now, he should be in from working or at least I hope so. *Crap!* I remember that he's gone with his dad to the sale. He might be gone all night. I send him a quick text and finish getting ready. I can't wait to see him Thursday, even if it's not under the best circumstances. Any moment I spend with him is better than nothing at all. When he replies, a smile spreads across my face, but it doesn't last long because I hear a light knock at my door.

"Come in," I say as I turn around and stand in shock when the door opens. Cash Money is standing before me with a bouquet of wild flowers. "I...I..." is all I can utter.

He takes a step closer as he hands me the flowers. The smell of fresh-cut flowers mixed with his recently showered scent is enough to drive me crazy. Taking the flowers from him, I manage to speak, "They're beautiful, but I thought you had to stay home."

He gives me a smirk as he answers, "Let's just say I have to be back really early tomorrow, but the thought of seeing you for even just a minute was better than none at all."

Throwing my arms around his neck, I say, "I love you, Cash Money. I love you with all my heart!" Happy tears begin to fall.

His lips press against mine, and he replies between kisses, "I. Love. You. Too."

"Ohmygosh! I just can't believe you're here!" I squeal.

"Well, believe it! I'm gonna hold you tonight just like you needed, but I have to be back home by six a.m."

"Cash! That means you'll have to leave by four-thirty!"

"I know, but *we* are worth it."

"Damn right, we are," I say as I devour his lips one more time before being interrupted by Caroline who doesn't even bother to knock.

"Oh, shit! Um…sorry, y'all! Hey, Cash! Um…" She turns and closes the door. The mood is now ruined, but the night is not. This is going to be a fabulous Friday night. I've got the love of my life, Club Purple, and the Kluft girls. Now, if only my best friend and the love of her life are safe, my night will be complete.

Chapter 24

Tori turns up the stereo as the music begins to pump through the hallway. Cash and I have yet to venture out of my room, but I'm about to starve. I'm pretty certain all the pizza is gone, or if not, it's some nasty supreme! *Yuck!* Surprisingly, they have saved me a few slices of pepperoni that Cash and I share.

"It's not a famous PB&J, but it will have to do," I say playfully.

As the nighttime hour begins to roll around, so do the people. Anyone that is everyone on campus is here. Tori and Caroline use their rooms to hide the booze. Just as things are starting to crank up, Mr. Wannabe Cop strolls through.

"Ladies, I'm afraid I'm going to have to shut it down," he says.

Anna turns on her charm as she approaches him. "Oh, Officer, please don't ruin our fun! We've worked so hard on Club Purple!" She then gives him a pouty lip. We all look at each other and almost burst at the seams.

He falls right into her hand. "Well, I guess I can let it slide for now, but by midnight, I want the music off."

"Yes, sir," she replies and bats her eyelashes.

He strolls through the room and stops directly in front of Tori's room with the door wide damn open. *Shit!* "Whose room is this?" he demands.

Tori starts to speak, but Anna comes to her rescue. "Mine. Oops. Guess we should hide that better."

"I believe that you should. I will, however, let this slide if I can get one of those to have as soon as I'm off duty." He points toward the beer.

"Sure! But you know you can drink it on duty, and we won't tell a soul," she whispers with a wink.

He takes the beer, slides it into his pocket, winks at Anna, and makes his way out of the dorm.

"Y'all are *bad*!" Cash states with his arms crossed.

"No, she is bad," Caroline says, "but it sure is nice to have her around!"

"Hey, is that all I'm good for?" Anna asks with her hands on her hips.

"No, you're good for getting free beer, too!" Tori exclaims.

"I always get what I want!" she says as she sways down the hallway toward a baseball player that has her name written all over him. He doesn't know what he's about to get himself into.

Club Purple is a night full of music, laughter, fun, drinking, and forgetting about what the future holds. By eleven o'clock, we can't even move down the hallway. Couples are bumpin' and grindin' to the music, people are making out against the walls, and the Kluft girls know that we have pulled off the dorm party of the year.

Cash and I never leave each other's side; we dance, laugh, and make out like every other couple in the hallway. The fact that I know he has to leave soon makes me sad, and he must read it on my face.

"Char-coal, don't be sad. Be glad that we are here in this moment."

"Oh, I am, but I don't want it to end," I say as my hands slide up his washboard stomach.

"Me either. Just think. This time next week I can spend as much time with you as possible."

"Now, how am I gonna finish the semester with you as a distraction?" I ask.

"Oh, so now I'm the distraction? I thought it was the opposite way around." That's when the stereo begins to slow, and we hear our song. We stop, look toward my friends, and then look back to each other. We forget that there are others around us, and we dance like no one is watching. Before the song ends, we are brought back to the reality that we aren't alone when some jackass yells for us to get a room, and that's exactly what we do. We make our way to my room and close the door.

186

Now, I have Cash Money all to myself for the next couple of hours, and I plan on using that to my advantage.

As the door shuts, Cash uses one hand to lock the door while the other continues to hold me close to him. With no chance of interruption, Cash and I fall deeper and deeper in tune with each other. Every kiss of his is met perfectly with a kiss of mine. We don't talk, but tell each other exactly what we are feeling with our physical movements.

Cash teases me, and I tease him right back. I know in my heart of hearts that Cash isn't going to cross that line, so tonight I don't even try to force him. I play his game, and by the time we are finished playing, we are both out of breath and content with each other.

We lie on my bed and hold each other. As I look at the clock, I know that he needs to go to sleep. He has a long drive and day ahead of him. I'd never forgive myself if something happened to him. Before long, his breathing slows, and he drifts off to sleep. Glancing over my shoulder, I watch him, and it's the most beautiful thing I've ever seen.

At some point, I can no longer keep my eyes open, but I'm pulled from my sleep by the sound of Cash's alarm. He doesn't hit *Snooze*, but he does take a minute to hold me a little tighter before he slides out of bed and puts his jeans back on. He grabs a Choice Cherry Gold from the fridge and sits on the side of the bed.

Running his hand through my hair, he kisses my cheek. "I love you, Char-coal. Thank you for being my forever." He kisses me sweetly again before he stands.

Grabbing his hand, I pull him back to the bed, leaving him with a kiss he won't forget. Then, as quickly as he surprised me last night, he's gone, and my bed feels empty without him. I toss and turn until the sun begins to rise. I know there is no point in trying to sleep, so I do the only thing that can clear my mind. I pull out my swimsuit and toss it into my bag along with a towel. I knock on Georgia's door, and she answers half asleep.

"I'm going to the pool. I need to clear my head," I state.

"Hold on, and I'll go with ya," she says.

"You don't have to. I just wanted to let someone know where I was going."

"Nah, hold on. I'm going, too." Seriously, I don't need someone to go with me. I just want to clear my head, but if I have a tagalong, I'd rather have Georgia than anyone else.

I hear her stumble and then talk to someone. *OMG! I bet Tucker is in there!* She emerges from her room a little later.

"Who's in there?" I question as she shrugs her shoulders. "It's Tucker!" Her face turns bright red. "You know you don't have to go."

"I know I don't, but you need me. I don't care if you think I'm just tagging along. I'm not. I know you, Charley, and when something's on your mind, you swim to escape. There's only one problem. We don't have a key to get in. Wanna run instead?"

She's exactly right, and I don't have anything to add to her comment. We go back into our rooms and throw on running apparel before exiting the dorm. The air is cool and crisp as we walk outside and to the stoop. We don't talk as we take a few minutes to stretch and then begin at a slow and steady pace around campus. We spend the next hour running, breathing, and escaping what I have in my future. On the final mile of the run, Georgia breaks the silence.

"Char, you know I love you, right? I knew from the moment I met you that you'd be my best friend on campus, but this has got to stop. You can't keep doing this to yourself; it's not healthy. You can't worry about everyone else when you're the one that people should be worrying about."

I stop mid-stride. "Huh?"

"Charley, you are the victim here, and it seems to me every time something goes wrong, you are the one that tries to fix the situation. I know you miss Cash, and you don't want anything to happen to him, but he made that choice. He has to live with the consequences. Piper and Joe have to deal with that issue as well... alone." As I start to interrupt

189

her, she holds up her finger. "I know you feel at fault, but you aren't. Dylan is. You need to accept that he's the problem, and nothing will be fixed until the judge is done with him.

I don't know what to say to her. I'm pissed, scared, happy, sad, and one damn bottle of mixed emotions about to spew like a shaken two-liter. Doing the only thing I know to do, I turn and continue to run. Georgia stays with me, well, maybe a stride or two behind me due to her height deficiency, but she doesn't leave me alone. Not for one minute.

When we reach the woods at the edge of campus, I take the path that Joe and I took not too many months before, and when I see the bench in the distance, I slow and then sit without saying a word.

Georgia doesn't say a word; she sits beside me and places her hand on my back to comfort me as I let all the emotions leave my body. I've said I'm done running, but it took Georgia telling me what everyone else was thinking to realize I'm not okay. I've always been one to hide my emotions and only let a few people in, but undoubtedly, the only person I've been fooling is myself.

When I have no more tears to cry, I sit with my head in my hands. She's right. I never realized that my way of controlling the situation was to control what happened around me, but when in actuality, I was the one that needed saving.

"Georgia, thanks for saying what needed to be said."

"Char, you're my dearest friend. I knew you wouldn't like it, but it had to be said. I'm here for you no matter what. No matter what you say about Thursday, it's gonna be hard; I'm here if you need me.

I shake my head okay as I stand. Together, we walk back to campus because I'm done running. Georgia goes back to her room to find that Tucker has left. For most people, it would have been a walk of shame, but we all know that he has nothing to be ashamed of as he walks across campus to his dorm. Georgia smiles as she sees her empty room: she knows she'll see him at Hank's tonight. Then, we both get ready for the day.

I spend the remainder of the weekend with the Kluft girls. We pig out, dance our asses off at Hank's, and sleep until lunch on Sunday.

When I wake up, I sit up quickly in bed. The first thought that crosses my mind is Piper and Joe. Wondering what happened, I text Joe. My phone rings almost instantly.

"Hey, is everything okay?" I ask with concern in my voice.

"Yeah, I'm just now coming home. What are your plans for dinner?"

"Nothing, I don't think."

"Okay, well, we need to talk. Meet me at my Jeep at five," he states.

"Is everything aight?" I ask as my nerves begin to increase.

"Yeah, it's gonna be fine. I just want to talk to someone about everything."

"Gotcha. Be careful."

We disconnect, and I call Piper. I can read her like a book, so I know I'll be able to tell if something is up. She sounds sleepy, but tells me about their night and about seeing Blanton. She doesn't hold back anything, and I can see how proud she is that Joe stood up for her, but also that everything is okay. We make a little small talk, and she tells me that she's coming home for support. I try to argue with her, but it's no use. She'll be there when I testify in court, and honestly, I feel relieved.

Looking at the clock, I have a little over four hours to spare before supper with Joe. I shower, look at my syllabi for my classes, and make sure I'm ahead of schedule. I want all my schoolwork done, so I can focus on Thursday. Thinking I should get a five-page paper for biology out of the way, I dive in and finish it within a couple of hours. It feels great to have it finished with time to spare. I send Cash a text to see if they are back yet, and he responds that they should be back late tonight. I let him know what little bit I know about Joe and Piper and that I'm having supper with Joe, and he tells me he will call as soon as they are home and settled. That won't be a moment to soon.

Trying to kill a little time, I make my way to Tori's room. She's studying for a biochemistry test. *Thanks goodness, I'm not a pre-med major!* Anna is watching TV in the room, and I make myself at home. After a few minutes, Tori finishes studying, and we watch reruns of *90210*.

"Dylan is so damn hot!" Anna says.

"Yeah, he is," Tori agrees, but doesn't say another word.

My face must say it all. Just the sound of his name has me motionless.

"I'm so sorry, Char. Luke Perry is so damn hot!" Anna corrects herself.

I try to smile, but it's almost impossible. Never in a million years would I have imagined that I would have reacted that way with just the mention of his name. I really must be losing it.

"It's okay. I'm not sure why it bothered me really because he is definitely not *that* Dylan."

After we finish watching the episode, I head to my room to grab my purse to meet Joe.

Georgia is on her way up the stairs as I make my way down. "Where ya goin', Char?"

"Supper with Joe."

Her eyes get huge. "Is everything all right?"

"I think so. I've talked to Piper, and she sounded good. I think he just needs to talk about it."

"Oh, okay. Well, if you need me, I'll be here the rest of the night."

As I walk out of the dorm, I see Joe already inside his Jeep. Looking both ways, I cross the parking lot and open the passenger side door. He jumps when I open it.

"Sorry, I didn't mean to scare ya."

"It's fine. I'm just tired and still trying to process this weekend."

"I can drive if I need to."

"Nah, I'm good. So, how does the BBQ Shack sound?"

"Fine by me," I say as I close the door.

We make our way to the little hole-in-the-wall BBQ place. There aren't many people here. They probably came for lunch. We find a seat, and the older waitress comes to take our order.

After she returns with our drinks, Joe takes a deep breath and begins to talk. "So, it went pretty well this weekend."

"And..." I know there is more. He wouldn't have wanted to leave campus without something else on his mind.

"I confronted Blanton. He was like a little puppy dog with this tail between his legs when I told him about Dylan getting caught. He apologized to Piper and her friends. He also told her to watch out for another group of guys in the area. Undoubtedly, they get their kicks drugging college girls and then leaving them as quickly as they find them."

"Great! So, other than that, did things go well?"

He begins to grin from ear to ear. "Yeah, they went *really* well. You're probably gonna think I'm crazy, though." With that statement, I'm a little scared to hear what Joe is going to say next. But, he doesn't talk; he takes something out of his pocket instead. It's a perfect square velvet box.

Ohmygosh! Ohmygosh!

"I love her, Charley," he says as he opens the box, and inside is a stunning emerald cut diamond ring sitting in the center.

"Joe!" I gasp and put my hand over my mouth. The waitress looks in our direction and has this excited look in her eyes. I hear her holler our way.

"Well, honey, are you gonna answer that poor boy or what?" Joe and my eyes dart back to each other before we burst out laughing.

"Ma'am, it's for my best friend," I correct her politely.

"She's one lucky girl! That is absolutely beautiful!"

"That she is," I say as I look at Joe. "So, is this what took you an extra hour to get home?"

"Guilty. Do you think I'm crazy?"

"It's like this. You know when you've found your forever. It is soon, but one thing that I've learned is that life is too precious to waste. Go after what you want, and live every moment to the fullest."

Letting out a huge breath of air, he responds, "Shewwww... I just knew you were going to tell me I was rushing things." The waitress returns with our food.

Choosing my words carefully, I reply, "I'm not saying I'd propose right now, but you will know when it's right... *and* when you ask her daddy."

Joe's eyes bug out of his head. "Ask her daddy?"

"Joe, you're wanting to marry a Southern Belle. Rule number one is to get her daddy's permission."

Joe looks a little pale. "I've only met him once. He'll think I'm crazy."

"Well, you are… for his daughter. He loves you. It will be aight," I tell him as I begin to eat my food.

"Squirrel, *really*? I have to ask him?"

"If you want her to say yes, you *have* to ask."

"Alright."

I laugh as I watch Joe try to eat. "It won't be that bad, I promise."

"I just don't know when I'd be able to do that."

"When the situation arises, you will know. Does she have a clue?"

"Nope. I mean, I know she feels the same way, and she mentions me when we talk about after college. This dad thing has me messed up. We don't do that up North."

"Welcome to the South, where the tea is sweet, and the girls are sweeter," I say in a thicker Southern accent.

He shakes his head as he takes another bite. Once we finish, we make our way back to campus. I'm glad that things went well this weekend. Joe informs me that he is coming to the hearing with Piper. I tell him he doesn't have to, but he insists, and says that she is picking him up on the way home late Wednesday night. I'm thankful for the support, but I'm not sure how I feel about it.

As I make my way upstairs, I'm so excited for Piper. Honestly, I have no idea how I'm going to keep my mouth shut about this, but I have to! When I arrive back to Kluft, everyone is watching a movie in Tori's room, so I join them. After it's over, we sit and talk about plain old stuff, and that's when Tori tells me that they are all coming Thursday.

"Um, y'all, I appreciate it, but I think I'd be better off with just the bare minimum. I don't want to sound rude, but it's gonna be hard enough with the people that have to be there. Plus, Joe said he and Piper are coming."

"Oh, so they can come, but we can't?" Tori smarts back.

I'm a little speechless. "It's just that I know my parents are going to be in a tizzy, and I don't want Mama to have to worry about anything."

"Charley! Did you think we were coming home with you?" Caroline exclaims.

"Well, yeah... isn't that what you were plannin'?"

"No, we are leaving early Thursday. We have better manners than that. We just want to be there to support you and Cash," Caroline continues.

"Oh, well then, I'd love for y'all to be there, but I don't know how much I will actually get to talk to you."

"We know, and that's okay," Tori says. "We love you, and we want to be there for you."

I nod in agreement and am embraced in a group hug. We watch a little more TV before heading back to our rooms. I'm on the edge of my seat waiting on Cash Money to call. When the clock approaches eleven, he texts and says he will call me around midnight, and that's not soon enough.

Doing anything to pass the time for the next hour, I go ahead and start to pack my clothes for my trip home. I stare at the closet. What does someone wear for court? Never in a million years did I picture myself walking into a courtroom, let alone testifying. After what feels like an hour, I finally begin to rummage through the closet. Starting with the essentials, I take a few everyday clothes, pajamas, and decide on two outfits for court. The first one is a pair of black dress pants paired with a baby blue blouse, and the other is an A-line back dress with the right accessories to match.

Glancing at my watch, I realize it has been all of twenty minutes. *Ugh!* What to do now? I pop in a movie and try to relax until I hear from him. Finally, a few minutes after midnight, my phone begins to blare "Crash My Party," and boy, do I wish he was crashing my party right now.

"Hey!" I say a little too excited.

"Hey, Char-coal," he says with enthusiasm, but I can hear the tiredness in his voice.

"How was it?"

"Good. We made a lot of money today, but I'm worn out. That traveling will kill ya," he says with a yawn.

"It probably didn't help that you didn't get much sleep last night."

"True, but it was totally worth it."

"Agree. Hey, Cash Money?"

"Yeah."

"I love you."

"I love you, too. I don't want to bring it up, but what happened with Piper and Joe?"

"It went well, but ohmygawsh, you're never gonna guess what happened when Joe and I went to eat supper... he's got a freakin' diamond for her!"

"He's what?! They haven't even been dating a month," Cash says with jealousy in his voice.

"I know, but you know as well as I do that you just know. When I told him he had to ask her daddy, he about died! I told him that it was the Southern thing to do."

"Yeah, when's he gonna do that?"

"I don't know, but I told him that he would know when the time was right."

Cash doesn't really respond. Instead, he talks about what he has planned for the next couple of days and asks when I will be home Wednesday. I inform him that I will be home by supper Wednesday at the latest, and he promises to meet me as soon as I hit the gravel. We exchange goodbyes and disconnect.

That night I toss and turn. I think about Cash and me, what this week will bring, and try to imagine what it will be like to face Dylan. Needless to say, I finally fall asleep as I see the sun beginning to rise. *Just great.*

At eight forty-five, I pull myself from my slumber and manage to get to class with a few minutes to spare. There's nothing like going to class in pajamas and a ball cap. I follow my normal routine to a tee, and by two, I'm ready to crash. I let Georgia know I'm going to take a nap, but I need her to make sure I make it to the café on time.

At exactly five, Georgia knocks on my door and then comes on in. "Hey, Char, it's time to eat." I mumble a response. "Char, come on."

Tossing back my covers, I take a second to look at myself in the mirror. *Ohmygawsh!* "Did I look this bad this mornin'?" I ask her. She just smiles. "Crap! Why didn't someone tell me? I mean, at least by noon anyways!"

"Char, I'm sure you didn't sleep well. It's no big deal. We all look like crap from time to time."

She laughs. "Now let's go. I'm starving, and everyone's waiting on us."

"Give me just a sec, okay?" I say still half asleep.

"Sure. I'll be in the hall," she says as she exits.

Looking in the mirror, I rub my hands over my eyes and yawn trying to wake up. I brush my hair into a ponytail and add a little blush and lip-gloss. Looking at my attire, I decide I might need something besides pajamas. Grabbing a pair of semi-clean jeans from the floor and a long- sleeved T-shirt, I change quickly and then slide on my Ariats and walk out the door.

"Girl! If only I could do that!" Georgia exclaims.

"Do what?"

"Throw something on and still look hot."

"Whatever. I just didn't think pajamas were appropriate supper attire," I say as we walk to meet the rest of the Kluft girls and eat.

Tuesday and Wednesday are typical school days except for the fact that I'm on the countdown to facing my nightmare. I meet the Kluft girls on Wednesday for lunch. We eat and laugh, but don't talk about tomorrow. Afterward, we all go our separate ways to finish our classes.

At two, I make my way back to the dorm to pack the last few items before I leave for Grassy Pond. When I get to the top step, I sense that something is off, but in a good way. Turning to look down the hallway, I notice that it has been decorated from end to end with random shit, and my door looks plum gaudy. That's when I hear music playing, and I see Caroline appear from her room. She is dressed in something that came from the thrift store or her grandma's closet, and she's singing "Don't Drop That Thun Thun" while dancing a little too crazy. I laugh as Georgia appears along with all the other Kluft girls. By the time the song ends, I'm in tears from laughing so hard.

"Y'all are too much!" I say.

"Hey, it's like this. We had to see a smile on that face of yours before you left," Anna states.

"Mission accomplished," I reply. "I love y'all!" We meet for a group hug.

"We love you too, Char! Now, go home to your Cash Money, and we'll see you in the morning when you take that SOB down!" Tori says firmly. *Nothing like her keeping it real.*

Georgia helps me finish getting the last minute items together, and I text Piper, Tessa, and Cash to let them know I'm leaving. As I walk down the hallway, my eyes begin to fill with tears. *Stop it!*

203

Everyone walks me to the stoop, and I tell them bye.

Getting into the Honda, I crank up the radio and try to push aside my sadness. This is the beginning of my forever. I just have to face my past head-on to accomplish it.

Chapter 25

The drive to Grassy Pond isn't too exciting. I spend the majority of the time singing country music to the top of my lungs. When "Famous" by Kelleigh Bannen comes through the speakers, I sing a little louder. That song holds so much home and meaning to what I did over break with Dylan. No, he didn't cheat on me, but what he did was way worse… and now he's famous in our small town. I hope no one ever forgets what he did to me.

When the song ends, I glance to my right and see a middle-aged gentleman looking my direction. I smile and burst out laughing. I know I looked like an idiot, but I don't care. Not to mention, it's probably better he couldn't hear my singing.

As the exit for Grassy Pond approaches, I turn on my blinker as the excitement of being home starts to rise. Within twenty minutes, I've hit every stoplight in town and can see the farm quickly approaching. Turning onto the gravel, I try my best to slow down, but I really just want to floor it.

When the house comes into sight, I can see every vehicle is in its place along with my favorite F250. A smile grows on my face, as I park my car and am greeted by my family and the ones I love the most on the front porch. Emerging from my car, I try to walk calmly to the porch, but that goes to hell quickly, and I sprint toward them all. Tessa and Mama take off toward me while Dad and Cash remain on the porch. *Why in the hell isn't he running?* Within seconds, Mama and Tessa are embracing me and not letting go.

"What's wrong with y'all?" I question. "Everything's okay, right?"

"Yeah, Char, it is. I think Mama's just a little emotional in general; she's been baking up a damn storm."

"Tessa! You watch that mouth," Mama states mid-tear.

Tessa shrugs her shoulders, and we make our way to the porch. I'm dying to be in Cash's arms, but something tells me that Dad is the one I need to hug first. Smiling at Cash, I give Dad a hug, and they tell me that supper will be ready shortly before they return inside the house. Tessa turns and gives me a wink like she arranged this entire alone time. She's a mess, but I love her.

"So..." I say as I place my hands into my back pockets, turning my head to the side and looking into Cash's eyes.

"So..." he says as he takes a step closer, sliding his arm around my waist to my back and pulling me close to him. As every nerve in my body comes to attention, I start to giggle, which catches him off guard. "What's so funny?"

"This," I say as I point between us. "I mean, it just feels like we're doing this for the first time."

"Don't you realize we are? This is the first time I've welcomed the girl of my dreams home, and the entire world knows. There's no hiding, crazy plans, or anything. It's just my Char-coal and me."

Placing my arms around his neck, I look deeper into his eyes. "The girl of your dreams, huh?" I ask as I brush my lips against his.

"Actually, you're not a dream. You're my reality and always have been, which is better than a dream."

"You steal my heart more and more each day, Cash Porter Montgomery."

"And you do the same, Charley Ann Rice." He wastes no time covering his lips with mine.

Forgetting the world is spinning around us, we are brought back to my front porch in Grassy Pond when we hear a throat being cleared. Cutting my eyes, I see my dad, and for some reason, I'm not surprised. I honestly think this is just a game for him.

"Aight, you two, supper's ready," Dad announces.

"Yes, sir," we answer in unison. Cash weaves my fingers in his and guides me to the kitchen for supper with my family.

We spend the next hour stuffing our stomachs until they are about to pop. Tessa wasn't kidding;

Mama cooked a feast. After supper, we sit and talk about school, the farm, and my plans for the rest of the semester. Tessa excuses herself to meet Dustin. Cash and I offer to do the dishes, but Mama quickly tells us to get out of here, so that's exactly what we do.

As we walk outside, the crisp country air tickles my face, and I stop to breathe it in.

"Char-coal, are you okay?" he asks.

"I'm fine. Just enjoying the moment." We stand there and appreciate the freedom within the moment, and at the ideal time, Cash takes me by the hand and leads me to his truck. I don't ask questions, but I'm safe with my Cash Money, and that's all that matters.

Guiding me to the passenger side, he opens the door and helps me in before closing it and hustling to the driver's side. I'm not close enough to him, so I slide to the middle seat. He gives me a wry grin before cranking the truck and driving away from the farm. I *wonder where we are going?*

As if reading my mind, he answers, "Char, we're going to the club in a little bit, but I just wanted to take a ride with you."

"It's your night. Whatever you want," I say as I lay my head on his shoulder.

We ride around Grassy Pond, out to the edge of town, and back around. Just when I think that he's going to return to the farm, he surprises me by going to Dixon High. *Now, I'm confused.* Pulling into the student parking lot, he parks in his old spot and turns off the engine.

"Char-coal, do you remember the last time we were in this spot?"

Taking a minute, I recall an abundance of memories of this spot, but the last time we sat here like this was the last day of Cash's senior year. Our birthdays are a little over a year apart, and he was always one step ahead of me. It worked out to my advantage for tests, figuring out teachers, and having someone that had been there already. But... the last time we sat in this spot... that was the moment I knew Cash loved me.

"Yeah, I remember," I answer softly.

"Whatcha remember?" he asks as he turns to look at me.

"I remember the final bell ringing for summer and hurrying to catch my ride home. I wonder who that was?" I say sarcastically. "But, when I got out here, you were talking to Dylan."

"And..." he says, probing for more.

"Y'all both looked like you were up to no good. I had been seeing Dylan for a few months, and you knew Dad didn't allow him to bring me home. He only let you. You gave Dylan and me a moment before I came to get into the truck, and then you said words that pissed me off back then."

"What did I tell you, Char-coal?" he questions as he holds my hand.

Taking a moment to think of the exact words, I feel my stomach begin to churn. *Ohmygawsh! Cash knew!* "You said that you didn't trust him as far as you could throw him and to watch out for him. You said something about him being a guy with a hidden agenda, and I thought you were being an ass." I feel the heat begin to rise, as I look Cash dead in the eyes. "Did you know he was like that?" Cash doesn't answer. "I *said* did you know he was like that?"

"No, Char-coal, I didn't really know. You know guys talk, and I had heard he was a take what he wanted kinda guy, but I didn't know anything for sure. I just had a really bad feeling about him. Every time he talked to me about you, it was almost as if he was digging for information or that he was trying to replace me. That day he pretty much told me you were going to put out for him, and I let him know real quick you weren't like that. That's what you walked up on. I should have done more to protect you."

"Why didn't you tell me?" I ask as I place my hand on his strong forearm.

Turning to look me in the eyes, he answers, "Do you really think you woulda listened? You were stuck so far up his ass it was ridiculous. I loved you with my whole heart, and there was no way I was going to lose our friendship over a battle I couldn't win back then."

Taking a moment to myself, I don't answer him. The thought that Cash knew in his heart that Dylan was going to hurt me kills me a little inside. I'm not going to say I blame him for any of it. All those choices were mine, but I just wish I wouldn't have been so crazy in love with the devil himself. Finally, I tell Cash what I think.

"Now that I look back on it, I realize how much you loved me, but I don't like the fact that you knew he was gonna hurt me. I mean, I understand. I wish I wouldn't have been so stupid, but bless, you dealt with all my wanna be with Dylan Sloan moments, stayed by my side, didn't kill him about the incident, and I left you! What guy lets a girl do that to him?"

Looking into my eyes, Cash answers, "A guy that's madly in love with a girl. I've known you were my forever since the day you bet me a PB&J dinner if you caught the bigger fish. I lost, and we've made PB&J's our traditional meal ever since."

Sharply, I reply, "Cash, we were twelve. You knew then?"

"Yeah, I've always known that you were more than just my best friend, but in that moment, you stole my heart and the biggest fish in the pond. I knew I had the perfect girl for me, and I'd be damned if I let you go."

"But, you did… you let me go," I say in a whisper.

Before taking my hand, he grazes my cheek. "Char-coal, I never let you go. Instead, I let you grow your wings and fly. I've been beside you every step of the way. Sometimes I wanted to shake the hell outta ya, tell you exactly how I felt, and grow a pair, I guess you'd say. Hell, some people probably think I'm a softy for letting you do it, but I know you. The more you push, the farther you run, and I never wanted to be far when you chose to run back to your forever."

"Don't ever let me run again," I say as I eliminate the distance between us, and happy tears begin to trickle down my cheeks as our lips meet. We now have a new memory that's about us, and no one else. Between kisses, I whisper to him, "Can we get outta here?"

Without a word, he turns on the ignition, and almost as if someone's looking out for us, our song comes through the radio. "Hey, Cash Money?" He looks at me. "You know you can crash my party anytime, right?"

"Oh, I plan on it." He puts the truck in drive, and we make our way to the club.

As we reach the club, I notice a car behind us. "Cash, do you see that?" I say with fear in my voice.

"That car? Yeah, it's made every turn with us. I just thought they might be going on down the road," he says, trying to shake away my worry.

Looking at him like he can't be serious, I ask, "What are we going to do?"

"I guess I'll stop at your parents and see if they follow us."

"Or we could call the police? I don't want any trouble tonight," I state.

"Me either. Let's just see who it is." Cash pulls to the edge of my gravel driveway before waiting for the car to pass, but we realize all too quickly that it's not going to pass. We can see Trent in the driver's seat. *Shit. Double Shit.* Cash looks at me, and I call my dad.

Within seconds, I see Dad's headlights coming our way. Cash goes to open the door, but I stop him. "Please don't." He shakes me off and steps out of the truck. I hear another door slam and see Trent standing in front of Cash, trying to act like he's someone with power. Cash keeps his ground, though. The closer that Dad's headlights approach, the louder Trent gets, and the harder my chest beats out of my chest.

"Hey, Trent. What's goin' on?" Cash asks in a friendly manner.

"I think you know damn well what's going on." Trent seethes through his teeth.

"Nah, I really don't know why you're tore up out the frame and following us."

"I know what you did. I know that you tried to make me look like a fool. There ain't no way in hell I'm going to jail over some stupid girls."

"Dude, seriously, you're not going to jail. Yeah, you have been doing some stupid shit, and Dustin and I have played you like the fool you are, but nothing's gonna happen if you get your shit together. You're a good guy and all this stuff y'all been doing is crazy. Don't you wanna make something of yourself? Get outta this town?"

Trent just laughs wickedly at Cash. "I'm never getting outta this town. None of us are. You know that as much as I do. Look at you just working on the farm with Daddy. Yeah, that's real grown up."

"I don't even know why I'm talkin' to you right now. *This* makes no sense," Cash says as he remains calm.

As they continue to banter back and forth, I see Trent pull something from his coat. *Ohmygosh, no!* Quickly, I dial 9-1-1, asking for the police because nothing good is going to come of this.

Unable to hold myself back, I jump from the truck. "Cash, watch out!" I scream as Trent points the gun at me.

"You little bitch! You couldn't leave well enough alone. You had to tell Blanton what was going on, too! How the hell am I supposed to make a living? Dylan should have left you alone before y'all even started." I stand frozen and hear my dad's truck turn off.

"Son, I suggest you put that away. There's no need in all of that. Put it away, get into the car, and never look back. We will forget this happened, but if you pull that trigger, I'm beating you to it," he says with his shotgun cocked and aimed directly at Trent. "What's it gonna be, Son?" Dad asks as he steps closer. We can hear sirens in the distance. Trent slowly drops his gun before stepping toward the car.

As three police cars approach the farm, Trent speeds off, and Dad puts away his gun. All but one pursues him. The last officer stops and questions us. Once he has enough information, he leaves.

"Charley Anne, are you okay?" Dad asks me before looking at Cash for confirmation that he's okay as well.

"Yeah, I'm okay. We're just getting ready to go to the club," I inform him.

"Like hell you are. Not after that. Y'all can go to our house or the Montgomery's, but you're not

215

going out there alone tonight." Disappointment spreads across Cash's face. "Cash, I didn't say you had to leave. You're just not taking her there tonight." *Did my dad just tell Cash he could sleep over?* "I'm no idiot, but I trust you both. Tomorrow's a different day for all of us, and if it was your mama and me, I wouldn't leave her for a minute." Hearing my dad compare us to mom and him warms my heart.

Rushing to my dad, I hug him tightly. "Thank you, Dad! I love you."

"I love you, too. Now, Cash, call your parents, and y'all get to the house."

"Yes, sir," Cash replies.

Once the truck is in Dad's view, he goes inside, and Cash calls his parents. Then, we make our way into the house. I have to say that this is the weirdest feeling I've ever experienced. Never in a million years would I have thought my dad would have allowed Cash to spend the night. We take a few minutes to talk to Mama and Tessa, grab a snack, and then go to my room.

Tessa is hot on our trail. "What the hell happened out there?" she asks. I give her a brief play-by-play, and she tells us about her night with Dustin as she makes herself comfortable on the floor in my room.

"What are you doin'?" I ask her.

"You didn't really think Dad was going to leave you two alone all night, did you?"

"Well, yeah, I did," I state confidently.

"You're right. I just wanted to see your reaction." Throwing a pillow at her, she ducks, sticks her tongue out, and then makes a break for her room.

Cash and I laugh as I fall comfortably into his arms. We watch my favorite movie and drift off to sleep as soon as the credits begin to play.

When the sun starts to rise, Cash begins to stir. He has his own internal alarm clock. "Char-coal, I gotta get home," he says as he moves my hair from my face.

"Really?" I pout.

He looks at me like I can't be serious. Then, it hits me, and I jump up. Today's the day. My breathing begins to increase, and panic sets in.

"Hey, it's okay," he says as he pulls me to his chest, and I take slow, deep breaths, and savor the last few moments I have with him. As he kisses the top of my head, I pull away and look at him. "Don't do that. It's going to be okay."

"I know, but I'm scared for all of us."

"There's no reason to be scared. I'll be there for you, and you'll be there for me. Remember we're in this together… forever."

Cash and I spend a few minutes together in silence before he makes the first move to go home. While trying to hide my emotions, I don't cry, but leave him with a kiss that says it all.

"I love you, Charley Anne Rice, and when today is over, I plan on never leaving your side."

"I love you more than life itself, Cash Porter Montgomery." I walk him downstairs and to his truck. After backing away, I try not to watch him drive away. This isn't the last time that he leaves my driveway, but it is the last time he will leave with a possibility of not returning.

I see him turn toward his farm and continue to watch until I can't see him anymore. I stand there motionless, watching the dust settle on the road until arms embrace me from behind. Turning, I know that it's Tessa, and I fall apart in her arms once again.

Chapter 26

Tessa pulls me to the porch swing, and we sit as I cry. She doesn't say a word; she's my rock. When I feel that I can't cry anymore, I wipe the tears on my sleeves. "Thanks, Tess."

"I'm your sister. I'm here no matter what is going on and whether you are right or wrong. Now, I smell bacon. Are you ready?" Laughing, I shake my head yes, and we go inside for breakfast with Mama and Dad.

After breakfast, I go upstairs, shower, and get ready for court. Looking at the two outfits I brought home, I choose the A-line dress. Rummaging through the closet, I find my black pumps and pray that I can walk in them. Taking extra time to finish my makeup and hair, I try my best to look like a professional. I want people to take me seriously and know this isn't a joke. After adding my waterproof mascara, I take a step back and like what I see. I grab my purse and make my way downstairs.

Tessa, Mama and Dad are waiting on me. "Charley, you look beautiful," Mama says.

"Is it too much? I want to look professional."

"I think it's perfect," she says. We make our way to the truck, and I send Cash a text.

Me: We're on our way. I love you 4ever & ever

Cash: We r 2! I love you 4ever & ever & ever

As I put my phone into my purse, I try my best not to think about the shrinking distance between our farm and the courthouse, but before I have much time to process it, Dad is parking. Tessa squeezes my hand, and I smile at her.

Dad cuts off the engine and speaks before opening the door, "Whatever happens in there today, remember why we are here, and that we are a family. We will get through whatever is thrown our way. I'm proud of you, Charley. One thing I want you to realize is that they might not get to Cash's case today. It's up after Dylan's, but they have to get a jury and everything. Just be prepared that this could go on for a while."

He opens the door, and we all follow. Mama puts her arm around my shoulder and gives me a squeeze as I step toward the curb, and Tessa takes my hand as we make our way up the courthouse steps.

As we enter the courthouse, we are met by a large metal detector and an officer. Dad empties his pockets, and we all follow in line, making it through with no problems. We walk down the hallway to the courtroom.

An officer opens the door for us, and an eerie feeling sweeps over my body. I see Dylan's family seated behind the defendant's side. They don't smile or look my way. Dustin looks at Tessa and waves to her. Today he has to stay by his brother's side, and she knows it.

We walk and sit behind the prosecutor's table, and I do everything I can to keep my mind off what is about to occur. The clock on the wall reads eight forty-five, and I know I have fifteen minutes until my case begins.

Bouncing my leg up and down, I'm brought to an abrupt halt when Cash places his hand on my shoulder. "It's gonna be aight. I have to go back there and wait until it's my turn, but I'm right here," he says, pointing to my heart. He kisses my cheek before the officer guides him out of the courtroom and into the holding area.

As quickly as Cash vanishes, the door opens, and Dylan appears. He is dressed in a charcoal suit with a white dress shirt and pale pink paisley tie. Not one tattoo is showing, and his hair is combed neatly in place. Even though he looks well put together, something is different. The swag that he usually possesses isn't there; instead, I see a scared little boy who looks at me with pleading eyes.

Refusing to look at him, I turn toward Tessa. She looks at Dylan with a *go to hell* look and squeezes my hand tighter. I can't help but feel sorry for Dylan. I know he's an ass, but he has totally fucked up his life because of one mistake. Thinking back to when we were younger, he was the kid on the swim team everyone looked up to. He's always got what he wants and been the best at everything. I guess that's why he did what he did. It doesn't make it right, and I hope he has to pay one helluva price. I just wish the Dylan I used to spend hours at the pool with when we were nine was still around. He was a *good* person, and I'm not sure what happened. He's the perfect example of a kid with a great family, support, and everything going for him, but one choice cost it all.

Dylan walks by and takes his seat by his lawyer. His dad places his hand on his shoulder for comfort, and we all sit and wait. The clock seems to be frozen in time.

At exactly nine, a petite African American woman walks proudly into the courtroom. We stand as she enters and then take our seats. She announces the case, and my stomach is full of butterflies. One by one, people are called and questioned at the stand. Slowly but surely, the twelve jurors are chosen, and we take a ten-minute recess before it's show time.

I don't leave the courtroom; I stay seated, waiting anxiously. I have no idea how quickly my name will be called. Checking my phone, I look for something from Cash, but who am I kidding? They probably confiscated his phone.

As I drop my phone into my purse, I hear voices that warm my soul, the Kluft girls. "Girl, you look all pro-fess-ion-al!" Hayden states. Only she would make light of this situation, but I love her for it. I stand and turn to face them as Georgia embraces me, and everyone else follows suit.

"Thank y'all for comin'," I say.

"There's no way we weren't," Tori states. "You are a part of us, and we are here for you."

Glancing at the clock, I don't have much time before the trial starts. The girls take a seat, and I get ready to testify against Dylan.

As Judge Reeves calls the court into session, she reads the charges to the courtroom. "The State charges Dylan Randall Sloan with second-degree forcible rape. What is your plea?"

"Not guilty," Dylan states with little emotion.

The State begins with their evidence against Dylan. After they lay everything out on the table, the judge asks if there is anyone they would like to call to the stand. This is my cue. When my name is called, I stand confidently, even though I'm a train wreck inside. I straighten my dress and walk with my head held high. Placing my hand on the Bible, I swear to tell the whole truth, and then I'm asked what happened that night in July.

"Miss Rice, can you tell us what happened on July 20, 2012?" the District Attorney questions.

"Yes, sir." Taking a deep breath, I begin to tell my side of the story. "My parents were out of town, and I was going to a party with Dylan, my boyfriend at the time. Nothing was out of the ordinary until we were on our way home. I became very incoherent and realized that something was off about Dylan. We had to leave early because of my responsibilities at the farm. When we got to the house, my sister wasn't there. Dylan took me to my room and raped me. I told him no several times, but it was like my body couldn't move."

As the DA paces the floor meticulously choosing his next question, I try to hold back the emotion from my voice. I want to be strong, but I'm unsure as he asks his next question.

"I have no further questions, your Honor," he says as he takes his seat.

When the State is finished with my questioning, I know that I'm now going to be put under fire with Dylan's lawyer, who is looking directly at me. He stands and walks slyly toward the stand as my body begins to quiver.

"Miss Rice, you said that Dylan drugged you. Is there any physical evidence to prove that? How did you know that happened?"

"I didn't feel right, and there was evidence of Dylan discussing those drugs on tape. I'm sure you're aware of those as well."

Pacing the floor, he turns to look at me. "I am aware, but aren't they from the same young man who beat my client?"

"Objection, your Honor!" the State yells.

"Objection sustained," Judge Reeves states.

Dylan's lawyer doesn't say anything to that. Instead, he pulls another stab at me. "Was Mr. Sloan not your boyfriend?"

"Yes, I believe I've already confirmed that," I say with fire in my voice.

"Why didn't you report this earlier?" he asks with a crooked grin that I'd love to slap off his face.

"I didn't know what to do. I didn't think people would believe me, but then I thought he might do this to someone else. I can't let that happen."

"Did you not try to take this into your own hands?"

"Yes, sir. I knew I needed proof to go to the police."

"In doing that, you put my client in harm's way, did you not?"

The State comes in with another disapproval. "Objection, Miss Rice isn't on trial."

"Rephrase your question or move on," the judge says with annoyance in her voice.

"No further questions, your Honor."

"Miss Rice, you may leave the stand," she says and relief washes over my body.

Over the next hour, the two attorneys battle out the evidence, give theories, and provide their final arguments. *Is Dylan not going to give his side? Seriously, is he that much of a pansy?* As I glance toward him, I'm shocked that he doesn't want to have the final word as usual.

Judge Reeves dismisses the jury for deliberation while the audience waits talkatively. After forty-five long minutes, the jury returns. This is the moment I've been waiting for. The spokesperson for the jury stands and hands the verdict to the bailiff who passes it to Judge Reeves. She gives no indication of her feelings about the verdict. She has one helluva poker face.

The spokesperson stands, and when asked, he reads the verdict. I feel the air still as I wait for the words. "The jury finds Dylan Randall Sloan guilty of second-degree forcible rape." He then takes a seat.

All the air expels from lungs, and relief washes over me. Tears begin to fall from my eyes. He's going to pay for what he did, but now, the question is for how long? Judge Reeves calls for order in the courtroom and gives her verdict. Dylan stands with his head hung low as he waits for his future.

"Mr. Sloan, I see that you have no prior crimes, but due to the nature of your crime, I'm sentencing you to one hundred and twenty months in prison. Your sentence is effective immediately." The bailiff walks to Dylan as he turns to look at his parents. Mrs. Sloan is a complete mess, and I lose it completely, too. As much as I hate what Dylan did, I hate to see his family suffer. My sister is in love with his brother, and they will always be a part of my life, but I can't help but wonder, what will happen when Dylan is released?

Mr. Sloan and Dustin try to comfort Mrs. Sloan the best they can and try to remain strong for Dylan. Dylan looks at me as he exits the courtroom, mouthing the words, "I'm sorry."

Doing the right thing, I mouth back to him, "I forgive you." I turn, and as a sob escapes on my sister's shoulder, the bailiff leads him into the hallway. *Why does my heart feel like it is being ripped from me again? I should feel relief, but instead, I feel pain filling my body once more.*

"Char, that has to be the most honorable thing I've ever seen. To tell him you forgive him? I couldn't have done that," Tessa says as she pulls me from her shoulder.

Wiping the tears from my eyes, I say, "I can't move forward without forgiving him, and neither can he. I know deep down in my heart that the good Dylan is in there somewhere. I just hope that he surfaces when he's released. Honestly, I feel like my heart has just been ripped out again. It's not that I love him or anything like that, but he was an important part of my life for a long time, even before we dated… it just hurts."

"You honestly amaze me, Char. Not many people can feel the way that you do, and I'm like you. I hope the Dylan we all used to love returns," Tessa says. Dustin and his family approach us.

"Charley, we are so sorry about everything. You know we love you, but he's our child," Mr. Sloan states with a wavering in his voice.

"I know. I just want everything to be like it was before all of this happened. I want Tessa and Dustin to be happy without this drama," I say confidently.

Pausing a moment, Mr. Sloan replies, "We do, too."

Court is adjourned for lunch, and after this win, I'm hoping that Cash's verdict goes in his favor, unlike Dylan's.

The Kluft girls are waiting outside the courthouse, and we all walk to the little café a block down the street for a quick bite to eat. Honestly, I'm not hungry, but I've gotta eat before this one, because if it doesn't go well, then I'm liable to swear off food forever.

"Charley, we're *so* proud of you!" Georgia exclaims.

"Yeah, you kicked ass up there!" Hayden says confidently, and of course, always keeping it real.

"Thanks, I guess," I reply, and we enter the small café.

At lunch, I'm pretty quiet. The Kluft girls and Tessa try to make me laugh. Piper and Joe eat with us as well. I looked for them while I was on the stand, but I didn't see them. Instead of keeping the thought to myself, I just blurt it out, "Where were y'all?" I state directly to Piper and Joe.

"Char, we were right outside. When they called your name, I just couldn't handle it! I couldn't watch you relive that again. I know that makes me a terrible best friend, but I just couldn't do it," Piper says, dropping her head.

"Oh, Pipe! It's okay! You're still my bff, and I understand. You've had a lot going on. It's okay, I promise," I say as I get up and hug her. We finish lunch and make our way back to the courthouse.

I feel confident as I walk back inside. I just pray that Judge Reeves sees that Cash was defending me, and that he gets to leave the courthouse when we do today. I feel as if I'm experiencing déjà vu, but instead of an asshole from my past, it's my forever on trial.

When we enter the courtroom, everything is the same, except for fewer people on the back row waiting to see if they are chosen for the jury. We don't sit on the right side like before; we sit on the

229

left beside Cash's parents. His mother has a tissue clenched in her hand and looks like she's barely holding herself together. I know this is hard, but there is something more. I can feel it in my soul.

Looking to Piper and Tessa, I know they will understand what I'm trying to explain without a word. Piper shrugs her shoulders, and Tessa, being the sister she is, doesn't wait or sugar coat anything as she whispers into my ear, "Char, you don't think…"

As I snap my head to look at her, my eyes widen, and I gasp as my heart sinks. "He's not!" I whisper in desperation and then look at Mrs. Montgomery. *Ohmygosh! I can't believe what I think is about to happen.* As my breathing hitches, everyone around me places their hands on me in comfort, and then my knight in an F250 and Carhartts appears, but today he's not in an F250 or Carhartts. He walks in with his head held high in a slim fit Kenneth Cole jet-black suit. His arms fit the suit perfectly, and his arm muscles hug to the fabric. His shirt is coral and it brings out his radiant eyes, and he's paired it with a matching tie. As very inappropriate thoughts enter my mind, I realize that if someone heard them I'd be charged with undressing him in public.

My breathing slows, and I focus on the most perfect man in front of me. He's a man, not a boy. He's willing to take life by the horns and deal with the consequences. He looks right at me and smiles that absolute smile that warms my soul. I nod and try my best to not think about the words I'm about to hear him say.

Tessa takes my left hand and Mrs. Montgomery takes my right. At one on the dime, the bailiff announces the return of the Honorable Judge Reeves. She comes in with poise, dominance, and power.

She takes a moment to look over the docket, and then Cash stands as the charges are read to him. "Cash Porter Montgomery, you are charged with assault inflicting serious bodily injury, a class C felony. How do you plead?"

Standing tall and proud, Cash answers confidently, "Guilty, your Honor."

Judge Reeves looks stunned, and his lawyer snaps his head toward him in shock. The spectators in the courtroom gasp, I bite my lip to hold back emotion, and Mrs. Montgomery begins to sob loudly. Mr. Montgomery does his best to comfort her, but is emotional as well. Cash doesn't turn to look at me, but I can feel exactly what he is feeling. This is his way of being a man. He did something that hurt someone, but he also did it because it was the honorable thing to do. For that reason, he will not lie because he is guilty of hurting the guy that hurt his forever. Rather than cry, I begin to smile. Once again, Cash has proven to be a man worthy of my love, and today is the ultimate sacrifice.

Judge Reeves takes a moment to gather her thoughts. "Mr. Montgomery, you *do* realize that you are admitting to these charges?"

"Yes, ma'am. I do," he says with even more assurance.

"Council, is there anything that needs to be presented to the court before I make my ruling?" she asks as she looks at them.

They both reply, "No, your Honor."

"Mr. Montgomery, is there anything you would like to say before I make my decision?" she asks with pleading eyes toward Cash.

"Yes, ma'am. I'm guilty. I did it, but if I hadn't, there is no telling what would have happened to Charley. Your Honor, she's my forever… do you have a forever?" She smiles and nods. "Wouldn't you do what you *had* to do in order to protect them? That's what I did. I know that I deserve to be punished, but Charley had been the victim for far too long."

"Thank you for your honesty. That doesn't happen often enough within these walls. We will take a ten-minute recess."

As she leaves, Cash turns to face us. "I'm sorry, y'all, but I had to do what was right. I'm not like him, and I will not lie. I take full responsibility."

Mrs. Montgomery has gotten her crying under control, and as he goes to hug her, the bailiff stops him. "Oh, sorry, I didn't know I couldn't touch them." The bailiff nods, and Cash looks at me. "It's gonna be okay. I know that it is; I can feel it."

Tessa speaks up, "Yeah, it's gonna be okay. I think the judge is a good person. She seems fair."

Hayden then pipes in as usual, "Yeah, she's got some spunk about her, but she seemed to react to you."

"React?" Cash questions.

"She smiled when you talked about your forever. I think she fell in love with Cash Money at that moment," Hayden says with a snicker.

"Lord, only Hayden would make light of this situation, but I wouldn't have you any other way," I tell her and then quickly turn when Judge Reeves re-enters the courtroom.

We sit and wait for what feels like an eternity, but when I look at the clock, it has only been one minute. Holding my breath, I wait for her to speak. *Hurry up! Just spit it out!* She asks for Cash to rise and takes a deep breath while crossing her hands.

"Mr. Montgomery, this is a Class C felony. You inflicted pain on another human being regardless the reason. You have a perfectly clean record, not even a speeding ticket, but you have to pay the consequences; therefore, I hereby sentence you…" I close my eyes and hold my breath, waiting for the harshest words possible. "to twelve months unsupervised probation. Case adjourned."

I exhale the breath and open my eyes, and a wave of emotions hit my body like a tidal wave. As the tears begin to fall from relief, happiness, and adrenaline, Tessa pulls me to her. Knowing I can't get to Cash Money at this moment, I look at him and fall to pieces in a good way.

At the sound of the gavel pounding the desk, I jump up and almost leap across the partition to Cash, but I don't have to leap far, because he meets me halfway. Embracing me in his arms, he presses his lips to mine then we hold each other tight and don't let go until his mama makes her way to her baby.

"Mama, I told you it would be fine. There was no need to worry. I spoke the truth just like you always taught me, and see where it got me… I'm free," Cash says with assurance in his voice.

"Well, not exactly," his lawyer adds. Tessa and I give an eye roll, and I turn to face my friends. They take turns hugging me and then excuse themselves outside. I stay back with my parents, the Montgomery's, Tessa, and Cash. Once his lawyer gives him the ins and outs of what the probation means, we exit the courtroom. Cash takes my hand in his, smiles at me with that perfect smile, and we walk toward our freedom.

Cash and I make a pit stop at the restroom, and when we are about to leave, we are greeted in the hallway by Judge Reeves leaving for the day. She looks our way and smiles.

"Thank you," I say to her.

"No, thank you, for having a man in your life that's not afraid to stand up for what's right. We need more Cash's in this world," she says as she exits the building.

Wrapping my arm around his, I walk closely with him. "You know she's right, don't ya? The world would be a better place with more Cash Money's."

He stops, turns toward me, and places his index finger under my chin. "Everyone needs their forever." He brings his lips to mine in the doorway of the courthouse. "Especially one that undresses the defendant as he enters the courtroom."

"Now, what gives you that idea?" I smirk.

"Knowing you since the age of four… that's how I know, but you know what? I thought it was hot."

"I bet you did!" I say as I pull him through the doors into the bright sunshine and toward the start of our forever.

Epilogue

"Georgia, I can't believe today's the day! I don't wanna leave ya!" I tell her as we finish packing my toiletries.

"I know. Honestly, I don't think I'm gonna make it through the summer without ya. You are comin' back next year, aren't ya?" she says with worry in her voice.

"That's the plan," I say with a smile.

"Good. If not, I'm gonna make a weekly trip to Grassy Pond for you and a burger from the Burger Shak."

We laugh, and I help her finish packing as well. Around eleven, Dad, Mama, and Tessa pull in with the truck. I'm beyond excited to see them and can't wait to be home, but I hate to leave the Kluft girls.

"Hey!" I say as I meet them all with hugs. "Cash really didn't come?" I ask them.

"Afraid so. His dad had to have him today. They tried everything to get it changed, but they couldn't. Cash being Cash couldn't let his dad do it alone," my dad informs me.

With sadness in my voice, I comment, "I guess I just thought he'd surprise me like he did before."

"Guess not!" Tessa states. Placing my hand on my hips, I give her the sarcastic *really?* look, and she laughs.

We spend the next hour loading everything into the truck. By then, all the Kluft girls' parents have arrived, and it is like one big family reunion. We joke about crazy things we did this year, what we are going to miss most about second floor Kluft, and then we are in tears by the time we finish.

"Y'all wanna grab some lunch?" I ask them. They all kinda freeze and look to each other for answers. "Um, are y'all okay?" I ask quizzically.

"Yeah, we just have a long road ahead of us," Anna says.

"I guess that's true; I forget y'all have farther than me."

As our parents make their way back to the cars, we take a few moments to say goodbye. We make plans to visit Georgia's beach house and to try to cross the Mason-Dixon line to see Hayden and Anna. If I do, that will be a first. We have a final big group hug, and we all are in tears by the time we go our separate ways.

As I prepare to pull out of the parking lot, I can't help but look back into the rearview mirror. This has been the roughest, yet best, year of my life. I discovered who I am as a person, what it's like to stand up for what is right, set goals and obtain them, and find a support system that will last a lifetime.

Just as I'm about to leave, I see Joe running toward the Honda. *How the hell did I forget to tell him bye? Maybe because I know I'll see him soon.*

Pulling my car to the side, I put it in park and jump out and walk toward him.

"You weren't leaving without telling me bye, were ya?" he asks with confidence.

"Um... no." I laugh. "I guess I'm just thinking about getting home; plus, I know I'll see you tomorrow."

"True. But actually, it will be next week. I'm driving back home tonight and gonna spend some time with Gran. Also, my parents want me to meet them to talk things out."

"Joe! That's great! I know they love you, and no matter what, I do, too!"

"Squirrel, you have a way with words, don't ya?" He laughs.

"You know what I mean! Piper, Cash, my parents, and of course, your Gran and I, all love you. You need to at least explain what they want to know. Who knows, it might be the start of *your* forever," I say with a smile.

Shrugging his shoulders, he replies, "Could be." He gives me a hug and tells Tessa bye before turning and making his way back to his dorm. I'm sure gonna miss him, but I'm glad to know he's part of my future, too.

Taking a cleansing breath, I put the Honda in drive, and we make our way toward Grassy Pond. Tessa and I cut up the entire way home. We get honked at by truckers and sing to the top of our lungs. I'm so lucky to have a sister like Tessa. She's one in a million, and I'll never take her for granted.

When we enter Grassy Pond, the smell of summer lingers in the air as we drive with the windows down. I get excited the closer we get to the farm. The feeling of home overwhelms my body, and I start to cry.

"Char, are you okay?" Tessa asks with concern.

"Yeah, I'm fabulous. I'm just glad to be home."

"I'm glad you're home, too. My workload is going to decrease a lot!"

"Yup, nothing's changed," I say to her with a laugh.

We all take turns unpacking the truck and Honda. When we unload the last box from the Honda, I make my way to my room. Taking a minute to collect my thoughts, I think about my freshman year. It's hard to believe it's over. As quickly as I made the decision to attend Southern, my first year has come to an end. I reflect on the people, memories, and experiences I had this past year, and then I think about this summer. I'm so happy to be home, but without the Kluft girls, it's gonna be rough.

I shake my head as I stare at the stack of boxes in my room. How in the hell did all this shit fit in that tiny room? I start to unpack when Tessa enters the room.

"Are you gonna help me or go missin'?" I ask her.

"What do you say we both go missin'?" she answers.

"Whatcha thinkin'?"

"I was thinkin' a little ride around the farm might be fun or going swimming at the pond."

I scan all the boxes in sight. I'm definitely not looking forward to unpacking, but procrastination isn't in my nature. Tessa gives me a look, and how am I to tell her no?

"So, which one is it… ridin' or swimmin'?" I ask her.

"Both."

"Aight." We grab a swimsuit and stop and talk to Mama for just a minute before heading to the barn to grab our four-wheelers. We spend the next hour ridin', racin', muddin', and just livin' life in the moment.

As we slow down on the lower end of the field, I glance at my watch, and Tessa knows exactly what I'm thinking. "When are they supposed to be back?" she asks.

"Around supper, I think." Cash went with his dad to a cattle sale a county over. I can't believe he didn't help me move home, but I think he just wanted me to spend the last moment with my friends and not focus on us.

"That's not too bad. Are you ready to go for a swim? You look a hot mess."

"Always keepin' it real. I might just start callin' you HJ," I joke.

"Huh?" she asks, confused.

"Hayden Junior," I reply.

"I like her, so I'll take it." She guns it toward the pond, and I follow right behind. As we approach the pond, I'm caught off guard when I see Cash's four-wheeler, and I give Tessa a puzzled look. She smirks and picks up speed. *He's back and didn't call? Something's not right.* The closer we get to the club, I notice Tessa trying not to laugh.

"You knew, didn't you?!" I ask as I slide off my four-wheeler and turn to look at her while wiping the mud off my legs and pulling my hair back through my ball cap.

"Who knows?" she questions with a shrug.

Not sure of what to make of the situation and wondering why Cash would have lied, I turn to face the club, only to be met by the most handsome man I've ever seen. Cash is propped against the club's ladder in a pair of Rock & Roll Cowboy jeans and a Memphis Snap shirt. His hair has been freshly cut, and his face is clean-shaven. In his hands, he's holding a bouquet of fresh daisies from his mama's flowerbed, and when he sees my mud-covered self, he grins and pushes off the ladder and begins to walk toward me.

I look back at Tessa, and she winks before taking off toward the house. It's obvious that I've been set up, but I have a feeling as long as it has something to do with Cash Money, I'll love it.

"Fancy seein' you here," I say as I get within speaking distance.

"Well, let's just say that I wanted to surprise ya."

"That you did, but look at me," I say as I point at the mud.

"Personally, there's nothing hotter than a girl that's not afraid to get a little dirty," he says as he hands me the flowers and kisses me gently.

"Thank you."

"Are you hungry?" he asks. "I made us supper."

"As long as it's PB&J's." I wink as we lace our fingers together.

"How'd you know?" He takes my hand and guides me to the ladder.

Taking the final rung, I am in awe when we enter the club. Cash has made our own private supper with candles, Choice Cherry Gold, and PB&J's on my mama's fine china. "Ohmygosh, Cash! You did all of this?" I inquire.

"Guilty."

"Don't say that again," I joke. "It's beautiful."

"Not as beautiful as you, Char-coal," he says as he takes a step closer, placing his hand on my cheek and pulling me in for a slow, heart-warming kiss. "I'm so glad you're home."

"Me, too." I eagerly try to meet his lips once again. He fulfills my request and holds me tightly. If I didn't know better, I'd think it was a goodbye hug, but I know we won't have any more of those.

"You wanna eat?" he asks nervously.

"Sure, but I need to clean up a little or at least wash my hands." He tosses me a wet rag and then I sit across from him at our private supper. He begins by pouring Choice Cherry Gold into wine glasses, and we fix our plates. During supper, we enjoy each other's company without interruption. We laugh, talk about what happened when I left the Kluft girls, what I want to do this summer at home, and I bring up the idea of transferring to be closer to him even though I told Georgia I'd be back. Of course, Cash loves that idea, but as always, he wants me to enjoy college.

As the sun begins to set, Cash plugs in his iPod and begins to play our song. Taking my hand, he helps me stand and pulls me into him, and we dance to our song in our club without a care in the world.

When it ends, he pulls me in for a kiss and then slowly pulls away. "I wanna show you somethin'," he says and points toward the ladder. Making our way down, he guides me to the pond. Taking in all the elements and checking every nook and cranny, I don't notice anything out of the ordinary.

"Everything's the same," I say.

Clearing his throat, he turns to me and takes my hands in his. "Char-coal, everything's the same. Since the first day we met until right now, everything has been the same. You and me. You have always been my forever regardless of the trials we have faced. This pond is ours, along with the club, and these memories that will never be tarnished or forgotten. I want to start our forever," he says as he pulls a little black box from his jeans and takes a knee. Opening the box, he asks the question I've been waiting my entire life to hear,

"Charley Anne Rice, I've loved you as long as I've understood what it means to love someone. You are my one and only, the one that gives me reason to breath, and I want to make you my wife."

Grinning from ear to ear, I can't help but answer him with one question, "Cash Money, what you wanna marry me for, anyways?"

Shaking his head as he stands, he replies, "So, I can kiss my Char-coal anytime I wanna." He doesn't wait for an answer; he kisses me with desire, hunger, and as if his life depends on it. Wrapping my arms around him, I fall deeper and deeper into his kiss, and then he pulls away abruptly. "I take that's a yes?"

"Yes, Cash Money!" I exclaim and then pull him back to meet my lips.

He pulls away one more time. "Don't you wanna see the ring?"

"Cash, I wouldn't care if it came outta bubble gum machine as long as you're the one that gave it to me."

Taking the ring from the box, he slides the carat and a half princess-cut diamond onto my finger. It's perfect. Once the ring is on my finger, I waste no time expressing my feelings to him. He lifts me off the ground and carries me back to the club. When we are inside, we focus on each other and enjoy being alone together.

"Tessa knew the whole time, huh?" I ask him.

"Yup, everyone knew, but you."

"Everyone?" I look at him with a wrinkle in my brow.

"Yeah, our parents, Tessa, Piper, Joe, and the Kluft girls all knew. I had to have all their permission."

"No wonder they were shooing me out of the parking lot! Those little huzzies! And Tessa let me look like this. I should have at least taken a shower before."

"Char-coal, I wouldn't have you any other way. Just think. It's a story to tell our grandkids one day, but if you wanna get rid of the mud, I know of a way," he says with a sly grin.

"Cash Porter Montgomery, are you suggesting we go skinny dippin'?"

"Maybe."

"Does this mean you're gonna break your promise?"

"Hell no, if I've made it this far, why stop now?" he asks with a laugh.

"Well, let's just see about that," I say with a wink as I shimmy outta my cutoffs and tank before jumping from the window. If I can't have Cash all the way yet, I guess skinny dippin' will have to do for now.

About the Author

Casey Peeler grew up and still lives in North Carolina with her husband and daughter. Her first passion is teaching students with special needs. Over the years, she found her way to relax was in a good book.

After reading *Their Eyes Were Watching God* by Zora Neal Hurston her senior year of high school and multiple Nicholas Sparks' novels, she found a hidden love and appreciation for reading.

Casey is an avid reader, blogger (Hardcover Therapy,) and now author. Her goal is to one day be an author who is recognized nationwide like Jamie McGuire, Colleen Hoover, Tiffany King, and Amanda Bennett.

When Casey isn't reading, you can find her listening to country music, spending the day at the lake, being a wife and dance mom, and spending time with friends and family.

Her perfect day consists of water, sand between her toes, a cold beverage, and a great book!

Website: http://authorcaseypeeler.weebly.com/
Facebook: www.facebook.com/caseypeelerauthor
Facebook Author Group: https://www.facebook.com/groups/219865574845739/
Twitter: www.twitter.com/AuthorCasey

Amazon: http://www.amazon.com/Casey-Peeler/e/B00FGJ1WFC/ref=ntt_athr_dp_pel_1
YouTube:
https://www.youtube.com/channel/UC0lmpt4hErNa
u1woOOsJOnw
Goodreads:http://www.goodreads.com/author/sho
w/7106874.Casey_Peeler

9-14

DISCARD

CPSIA information can be obtained at www.ICGtesting.com
Printed in the USA
LVOW07s1520090914

403215LV00002B/408/P